DEVOTED DEFENDER

DEVOTED DEFENDER

DANGER IN THE DEEP SOUTH #2

RACHEL DYLAN

Devoted Defender
Copyright © 2016 by Rachel Dylan
Ebook ISBN: 9781535257497

NYLA Publishing
350 7th Avenue, Suite 2003, NY 10001, New York.
http://www.nyliterary.com

God is our refuge and strength, a very present help in trouble.
Psalm 46:1

ACKNOWLEDGMENTS

A huge thank you to the members of my wonderful street team for all of your support, encouragement, prayers, and feedback. It's amazing to be on this journey with all of you.

I'd also like to thank Denise and Beth for your keen insights on this story.

As always, many thanks to my agent Sarah Younger and the Nancy Yost Literary Agency for your continued support.

CHAPTER ONE

Annie Thomas heard the sound of loud, male voices coming from the dining room of the Perry mansion. She'd left some recipe notes for a new soufflé in the kitchen yesterday. Even though she hadn't wanted to go back to the house on her night off, now had seemed like the only good time to drop by and pick them up so she could experiment on the dessert. She had a key to the Perry mansion, and they trusted her to come and go as she pleased. Being the personal executive chef to one of the most elite families in Atlanta had some perks.

Mr. and Mrs. Perry were supposed to be out at a charity event for the evening. But it appeared she was mistaken. Her boss, Doc Perry, and another man whose voice she didn't recognize were obviously arguing in the dining room. Something was wrong.

She paused, trying to determine what she should do. Move to another part of the house? Leave and go home? Call someone? Given her past, she couldn't call the police. That much she was sure of.

As the voices got louder, she could hear clearly that there was a major disagreement brewing between the two men.

"We had a deal," the deep male voice said. It was definitely not a member of the Perry family or their close friends. The Perrys did a lot of entertaining, but this wasn't a familiar voice to her.

"Yes. But one made to be broken. That's business," Doc said. "Simple as that."

Annie knew that Doc ran a highly successful business in addition to doing his philanthropic work. She couldn't help herself and took another step closer to the dining room.

"Can I speak freely?" the man asked Doc.

"Yes. The staff has the night off and my wife is out at an event. So whatever you have to say, get it off your chest."

"I don't think you understand who you're working with, Doc. No one breaks a deal with Tim Silva."

What kind of deal could Doc have made with this guy Silva? She'd never heard the name before. A chill shot down her back. She resisted the urge to flee although she didn't really know how much help she could be if a fight broke out between the two men.

"This is business. Tell Silva that it's not personal, but I'm no longer satisfied with the arrangement. It served its purpose for a while, but I never agreed to take these latest shipments. It's a change in the terms of what I was told to expect, so I'm ending things."

Doc was the type of man who was used to giving orders and having people comply. She peeked around the corner into the dining room but didn't recognize the man standing opposite to her boss. He wore a dark jacket with jeans and his blond hair was in a buzz cut. Given his size and build, he looked like he could've been a professional bodyguard. He towered over Doc.

"It's a package deal when you work with Silva. You're not done until he says you are. You understood that when you signed up, Doc. He gave you everything you needed. Now you need to help him."

"That's just not going to be possible. I'm walking away. As far as I'm concerned my relationship with Silva is over."

The man took a step closer to Doc. "It's not that simple."

"Of course it is," Doc shot back.

"Doc, the rumors aren't that you're looking to leave the business, but just the opposite. And what's even more troubling is that you're trying to move in on Silva's business."

"That's absurd," Doc answered quickly.

Too quickly. Annie had only known Doc Perry for six months, but it was evident to her that he was lying to the muscle-bound man. He looked the same way he did when he told Mrs. Perry that he hadn't eaten bacon for breakfast when he actually had. It struck her that Doc was up to no good, which was totally out of character. But she didn't know what she should do about it.

"You really expect me to believe you?" the man said. "I'm trying to give you an out here. Trying to help you. And you're lying to me."

"I told you. I'm done with Silva. That's all you need to know."

"I'm sorry, Doc. Are you certain that's it? You're finished?"

Doc nodded. "Yes, it is. I think you can see yourself out. We're done here."

Annie sucked in a breath as she saw the mystery man reach inside his dark leather jacket. Her world stopped as she watched the man pull out a gun, and, without hesitation, point and shoot her boss squarely in the head. The piercing sound of the gunshot reverberated throughout the ornate dining room.

Doc crumbled to the ground and bright, red blood flowed down the side of his face. Without thinking, she screamed. The blond man turned and looked—his blue eyes fixated on her, momentarily puzzled at her presence.

"Wait," he yelled. Then he pointed his gun at her. She was in big trouble. Instinctively, she turned to run away.

"If you talk or you go to the cops, you're a dead woman," the man shouted. "I'll hunt you down myself."

He kept screaming for her to stop, but there was no way she was going to. If she stopped, she'd be dead just like Doc. She didn't look back as she ran through the kitchen, down the hall, and out the front door of the house. Gunshots rang out in the night. Was he trying to scare her off or kill her? It didn't matter. Since she'd just planned on a short trip to pick up the recipe, she'd parked her car right out front on the street. That decision likely saved her life.

She had just witnessed a murder, but she willed herself to run faster. Her feet pounding the pavement until she reached her red Fiat and jumped into the driver's seat.

Not wasting another moment, she started the engine and hit the gas. She pushed back the wave of nausea that threatened to overtake her. Doc had been shot point blank right in front of her eyes. The blond man clearly had no remorse. No, he was there to do a job. A kill mission.

What had Doc gotten into? It sounded like it was something illegal. She didn't know whether the shipments referred to drugs or something else.

Suddenly she was very conflicted. Should she go to the police? And tell them what? She'd just witnessed a murder? A man she had never seen before was in the house and shot Doc Perry? One of the most well-known men in the fancy Atlanta suburb? What if they didn't believe her? Given her past, she didn't know if she could ever trust law enforcement again. Not when they'd abandoned her before. And even more, what about the threats from the shooter? He said he would kill her if she went to the police. No, it wasn't worth the risk right now.

Her eyes blurred with tears, but she gripped the wheel trying to focus on the dark road. She'd lost track of how long she'd been driving as she tried to pull herself together.

Suddenly headlights came up behind her, and she feared the worst. But when the large truck passed her and kept on going, she let out a sigh of relief. She was on edge and rightly so. Although just because that truck didn't mean her any harm, didn't mean she was safe. She still felt like she had a huge target on her back. She punched the gas going dangerously fast on the curvy back roads headed out of the Atlanta suburbs.

Dear Lord, please protect me.

She couldn't go to her apartment. It was far too dangerous. Her mind raced with thoughts. She had her small purse and a bag in the trunk with a few things she hadn't unpacked from her last trip to a culinary conference in Savannah. It wasn't much, but it was going to have to do.

One thing was certain. She needed a plan. A place to hideout until she could figure out what was going on back in Atlanta.

She drove into the night until she saw a sign for a town called Maxwell. *This is it*, she thought. She'd stop here for the night and decide tomorrow what her next steps would be.

When the red and blue flashing lights came up behind her, her heart stopped. Had the police already tracked her down? Did they want to question her about Doc's murder? No, that wouldn't make any sense. The only person alive who knew she was at the house tonight would've been the killer. But that didn't stop her from being worried.

She certainly couldn't try to outrun the cops, so she pulled over to the side of the road and waited for the officer.

Rolling down her window, her pulse raced as she looked up into a pair of bright blue eyes.

"Ma'am, can I please see your license and registration?"

She pulled her identification out of her little pink purse and registration out of the glove box.

Instead of questioning the handsome dark haired officer as to why he pulled her over, she decided to stay quiet and see how he played it. She didn't need to cause any more problems for herself.

He took a moment to look at her documentation. "Thank you, Ms. Thomas. Did you realize you were going sixty in a forty-five?"

She had gotten pulled over for speeding? Really? She let out a sigh of relief. This officer had no idea about the ordeal that she had been through tonight. He just wanted to give her a speeding ticket.

"I'm sorry, Officer. It's late and I'm not familiar with the area."

"What brings you to Maxwell?" He looked directly into her eyes.

She couldn't exactly say that she was on the run because she'd just witnessed a murder and also been threatened by the shooter. There was no time for indecision. "I'm actually looking to maybe stay in Maxwell for a bit."

"Really?" He quirked a curious eyebrow. "Where are you coming from?"

She didn't want to provide the direct answer. At least not yet. "I'm looking to spend some time in a smaller town. I saw the signs for Maxwell and thought it would be perfect." Well, that wasn't exactly how it all went down, but it was close enough.

He leaned in further. "Because you're new to this town, I'll give you a warning this time around. But if I catch you speeding again, I'll have to give you a ticket, ma'am."

"Thank you, Officer." She called as he headed back to his patrol car to do whatever paper work was necessary for the warning.

But when he came back to her window, he picked up right where they left off.

"You're welcome. Now where are you headed?"

"Actually if you could point me in the direction of the nearest hotel, I'd be grateful."

"The Maxwell Inn is just about a mile and a half down the road on your right. It's not too luxurious, but it's clean and comfortable."

"That sounds perfect."

"And, ma'am."

"Yes?" Her heart pounded as she prepared for what he was going to say next.

"I'll lead you there to make sure you find it. Just follow me."

"Thank you."

He walked back to his car. Would running away to Maxwell bring her the relief she needed or just make matters worse?

* * *

The next day, Chief of Police Caleb Winters walked a few blocks from the station down to Pa's Diner to grab his usual lunch. But he still couldn't shake the feeling that something was wrong with the woman he'd pulled over last night. She'd been on his mind the rest of the evening and this morning.

There was something about the look in her hazel eyes that made him think there had to be more to her story. Yeah, she'd been speeding, but when he stopped her, there had been fear in her eyes. Was she in some sort of trouble? Regardless, he felt the pretty brunette was hiding something. Maybe he was always on alert because of his time in the military.

He had run her license and registration, and they had checked out. But why was this woman in Maxwell? People didn't just drop into a town like Maxwell. If she were up to no good, he'd figure it out. And if she were in some type of trouble, then he'd be there to help her. His family always told him he was a fixer. From a young age, he wanted to solve people's problems. And it wasn't just people, as he was reminded often. That's why he currently had two dogs at his house that had been dropped off as strays at the station. He refused to take them to the pound where they likely would've been put down.

Pa's Diner was one of the busiest restaurants in town. The all-day breakfast and late night diner had something for everyone. Including his weakness—a greasy BLT. He figured one day he would have to stop eating them for lunch, but it wasn't that day yet.

He walked into Pa's, which was just off the town square, and took a seat on one of the barstools.

Jen Spencer walked over with a smile. "Your regular, Caleb?"

He'd known Jen since elementary school. The sweet, single mom worked the day shift at Pa's while her daughter was in school.

"Yeah, Jen. That'd be great."

"We'll have to see how it tastes today. We have a new cook working that just started this morning. You know Joan's back surgery has her down and out for a bit and we haven't found a good replacement yet. Just different people here and there helping out."

"I'm sure it will be fine." How hard was it to make a BLT? He could even make one, and that wasn't saying much, given his culinary skills. He was great with a grill, but that was about it.

He drank a gulp of sweet tea and waited for his lunch to arrive. He scrolled through his phone but there were no pressing messages. Sometimes he wondered how it would be to work in a larger city with much more action. But he loved Maxwell. His family and his entire life was this town.

After the big trial last year that had embroiled Wakefield Corporation, one of the towns biggest companies, he had welcomed a period of calm. He trusted that God would let him know if he was supposed to search out something else. And for now, he felt he was in the right place.

A few minutes later, Jen came back and set his food down in front of him. "What is this?" he asked.

"That's your BLT." Jen smiled.

He looked down at the sandwich that didn't look anything like his normal BLT—which was usually smashed down dark toasted bread with tomatoes oozing out the sides along with the bacon strips.

"Give it a taste and let me know what you think," Jen said.

He was hungry so he didn't let the fancy looking presentation deter him. He picked up the sandwich and took a big bite.

There was a cheese on it that had a strong flavor, and the tomato had been fried. There was also some kind of sauce. He was a creature of habit, so he didn't want to love it. But man, it tasted good. "Wow," he said. "This thing is amazing. I don't know that I'd call it a BLT, but whatever it is, it's awesome. What kind of cheese is this? And the sauce?"

Jen patted his shoulder. "Let me bring out our new cook and you can ask her."

He glanced down at his phone and when he looked back up he was staring into Annie's hazel eyes.

"Ms. Thomas," he said.

"You two know each other?" Jen asked.

Annie cocked her head to the side. "The officer pulled me over last night when I got into town."

Jen laughed. "This isn't just any old officer. This is our chief of police, Caleb Winters."

A flicker of worry shot through Annie's eyes before she smiled.

"As long as you abide by the speed limit, you won't have any problems from me."

"We were fortunate that Mary Ann at the Inn sent her our way first thing this morning, and we put Annie right to work." Jen smiled and then turned around. "Gotta go do coffee refills." Jen walked away to serve other customers, leaving the two of them alone.

"I didn't want to say anything in front of Jen," he said. "But are you sure you're okay?"

She placed her hand on her right hip. "Why wouldn't I be?"

"That wasn't really an answer. But people don't just pop up into our small town in the middle of the night like you did. It's unusual. So if you do need anything, I want you to know you can count on me."

"I know it may not be the norm, and I'm not from around here, but I want to be. Isn't that all that matters?"

Could he get through to her? "Well, if you're in some kind of trouble, please let me help you. It's what I do for a living."

"You didn't mention that you were the chief of police. What were you doing on patrol?"

"It's a small town. We all play various roles here. We don't have a big enough police force to pick and choose assignments. So I do what has to be done." He paused. "But you're still avoiding my question. Is there something wrong?"

"Don't worry about me. I promise I'm not going to cause this town any trouble."

He didn't know if he was so sure about that. "If you change your mind and want to talk, just let me know." He needed this woman to open up to him.

"Thank you. I should get back to work." She turned and walked back toward the kitchen.

She said everything was fine, but his gut told him otherwise. What was Annie hiding? Or even worse, who was she hiding from?

CHAPTER TWO

After a full day of working at Pa's Diner, Annie's body was aching from exhaustion. But her first day on the job had actually been fun. She thought it was going to be difficult to cook diner food, but it was actually freeing to be able to mix things up and also provide tried and true favorites.

She'd gotten a kick out of the responses from the customers. Almost every single one of them was full of compliments. It felt good and had taken her mind off of her problems as she focused on fixing food for so many people. Well, as much as anything would. She still had to figure out what to do. What happened last night weighed heavily on her.

The words of the shooter were still so fresh in her mind, but she also didn't think she could just sit back and hope that things would work themselves out. No, she knew better than that.

It didn't help that she felt like the chief of police didn't buy her story as to why she was in town. She didn't like explaining herself to anyone—and especially not a police officer who might start digging into her past.

She walked down the sidewalk of the town square, noticing a small coffee shop, a bookstore, and a craft shop on her right. On the left side of the street she saw a bakery and a hardware store.

The tranquility of Maxwell was a stark contrast to the battle raging in her mind. Even though she was tired, she was still determined to move forward. Doc's youngest son, Phil, lived right outside Atlanta in another fancy suburb. She and Phil had gotten along well from the start, as he was responsible for conducting her first interview with the family. Perhaps she should reach out to him. He wasn't directly involved in any of the family businesses, so if there was something illegal going on, he probably didn't know anything about it and deserved to hear what really happened to his father. Also, she had to warn him because now that she thought about it, he and the rest of his family could be in danger, too. She had no idea how widespread the threat could be. She felt some level of responsibility to act.

She hurried back to the Maxwell Inn, but didn't even go to her room. Instead she opted to get into her car and make the drive to see Phil. Looking down at her watch, she thought it would probably take her forty-five minutes to get there.

When she reached the large three-story brick house in the luxurious suburb it struck her how different this area was from Maxwell. She'd grown up with so little and never felt like she belonged in a fancy high-income neighborhood like this.

She pulled up into Phil's driveway. He was still a bachelor. And if she was honest with herself, she felt like Phil may have been a bit interested in her. But at the end of the day, he would never want to date the staff, and that was perfectly fine with her. She wasn't looking for a relationship. She just wanted the safety and security that being on her own afforded her. There was no place in her life for a man. Men had only provided her mother heartache and pain—why would her life be any different?

Annie walked up the brick steps to the front door and rang the doorbell. Unlike his father, Phil didn't have a full-time staff. And Annie was hoping that he would be alone.

Phil opened the door, and she immediately knew that things were wrong. Phil's blond hair was disheveled and his brown eyes were red. His blue dress shirt was wrinkled and only half tucked in. This was not the totally put together man that she knew.

"Annie, I'm so glad you're here." He grabbed onto her arms, pulling her through the front door and into the living room. "You must have heard about father?"

"Yes." She didn't want to get into details just yet. She wanted to hear what Phil had to say. And she didn't have a game plan here.

"I didn't know if word had gotten to you, Annie. Everyone has been so tight lipped and we've been able to keep it out of the media, given our family connections. But that's going to change probably within the next twenty four hours." Phil paced back and forth and then turned to her. "How did you find out?"

"What did the police tell you about what happened?" She turned the question back on him.

"They're saying it was a home invasion. Father must have let the guy in. But the strange thing is that absolutely nothing was stolen." He ran his hand through his hair. "I don't know what to think."

"Phil, I need to tell you something very important."

"What?"

"I need to know that I can trust you."

He led her over to the sofa. "Have a seat and talk to me, Annie. You know you can tell me anything."

She sat down beside him and took a deep breath. *Here goes nothing*, she thought. This was the right thing to do. He deserved to know what had happened to his father. "I was in the house the night your father was killed."

"What?" Perry's dark eyes widened in disbelief. "What do you mean? I thought that was your night off."

She nodded. "It was, but I ran by the house to pick up some recipe notes I'd left in the kitchen. And when I was there I heard your father arguing with a man. Someone I didn't recognize." She took a breath as vivid memories flooded back to her. But she had to get through this. Phil needed to hear the truth. "Then the man shot him."

"What? Why didn't you go to the police, Annie?"

"The shooter saw me. He threatened me." She fought back the fear that threatened to overwhelm her. She needed to get through this conversation. "Then as I was running away, he told me he'd kill me if I went to the cops."

Phil shook his head. "Did you hear the conversation between my father and the shooter?"

"Part of it. And that's one of the reasons I came to see you. I wanted to let you know that you could be in danger."

"What did they say to make you think that?"

"Enough to know that your father was doing business with some man named Tim Silva. And, Phil, I hate to be the one to tell you this, but it sounds like your father may have been involved in some illegal activities. I'm not sure exactly what type, but it didn't sound good. I'm sorry, I know this has to all come as a big shock to you."

While he was looking down, Phil let out a deep breath. But then as he spoke, his eyes were filled with sadness. "No, I'm the one who is sorry, Annie. You should have never been in the house last night."

Her heartbeat thumped loudly in her chest, and she stood up from the couch. "What are you saying, Phil?"

"I had hoped that what I was told was untrue. But now hearing it from your own lips—it's unavoidable. You know way too much."

The way Phil looked at her told her everything she needed to know. There was now no doubt in her mind that Phil was mixed up in all of this. And she'd just gone to him and offered herself up on a silver platter. Now what? "I think I should go."

"I'm sorry, Annie. I can't let you do that."

She took a step back and he stood, grabbing onto both her arms. She sucked in a breath at his tight grip on her body and tried to break herself free. "Please, Phil. You don't have to do this. Just let me go."

"It's better this way than if Silva's men get to you."

"I won't say anything. I promise." She had to keep him talking as she pulled away again. Try to figure a way out of this mess.

"You've already heard too much. You know more than you should. There's no way Silva will let you live. You've been marked."

"So what now? You're going to kill me? You're not a killer, Phil. That much I know." She tried to appeal to his humanity. A tear fell down her cheek. Was she going to make it out alive? How long could she keep him talking—long enough to plot an escape?

His grip loosened. "All I can say is that I'm sorry, and that it'll be fast. I like you, Annie, but you've crossed the wrong man. Now that I know about what you saw and heard, I can't have that hanging over me. If I just let you go, I'd be in trouble with Silva, too. I have a drug I can give you through an injection. You'll go to sleep and won't feel a thing."

Let him think that she would be compliant. Then she'd make her move.

He looked down at her. "Just know that I never wanted you to get wrapped up in this."

She used the little amount of space he'd put between them to her advantage. With one smooth motion she brought her knee up into his stomach knocking the breath out of him. He reached out for her, and she screamed as she sidestepped him. This was it. If he was able to hold her captive and give her the injection, she'd be dead. He was tall and strong, and she didn't really stand a chance. Her basic self-defense class would only get her so far. But she wasn't going to give up.

He lunged toward her again, tackling her, and they crashed into the end table knocking over the lamp. She hit the ground hard and her vision blurred.

A gunshot rang out loudly. But it wasn't from Phil. No, he was running out of the living room toward the back door. What was happening?

She was a bit disoriented from being tackled to the ground. She blinked a few times as she lay there trying to compose herself.

"Ms. Thomas, can you hear me?"

She looked up into striking blue eyes. The ones that belonged to police chief Caleb Winters. And then her world faded into darkness.

* * *

Annie awoke and fear ripped through her body. Then she remembered what had happened. And now as she looked around it was clear that she was in a hospital. But was she safe?

"You're awake." Caleb's voice came from the side of the bed.

She turned and saw him there. "How long have I been out?"

"Overnight. Once they ruled out a concussion they gave you something for the pain. You had some nasty bruises and cuts."

"How...how?" she stuttered. "How did you find me?"

"I followed you."

Her first instinct was to be upset, but then she realized that if he hadn't followed her, she'd be dead by now. "Where are we?"

"A hospital outside Atlanta. I didn't want to risk taking you back to Maxwell last night without knowing the extent of your injuries."

"You saved my life. I don't know how to thank you." Regardless of her reservations about law enforcement, he had saved her.

"You can thank me by telling me what in the world is going on? What kind of trouble have you gotten yourself into? I can help you, but I need to know the facts."

"It's not that easy." How could she ever make him understand? Not just the facts, but why she reacted the way she did.

"Take your time. If you're not up to talking to me at this time, it can wait. You've been through a lot."

She knew at that moment that she had to have an ally, and this man had just saved her life. Yeah, she wouldn't normally trust a police officer. Not after she'd been betrayed by them in Florida. But this was more a temporary move out of necessity.

She thought she might have a little time before anyone figured out that she was at the Perry's two nights ago. But it's possible they'd want to question her regardless given her role as an employee. And if they found out she'd skipped town, that would make her look guilty. Or at least raise some red flags. And it actually worked out to her benefit that he was the chief of police and not a low level officer. She needed someone in a position of authority.

She looked up at him. He stood well over six feet tall with short dark hair and bright blue eyes. They were the type of eyes that could be trouble. But she wasn't looking for any more trouble right now. She had enough of her own.

"I'll tell you what I know. Should I call you Chief?" she asked.

"Caleb is just fine."

"I didn't know if I needed to address you by your title. Since you're chief and all."

He laughed. "We're not so formal around here."

"Then you should call me Annie." She paused. "I don't even know where to begin." And that was the truth. She wasn't going to talk about her past. But she knew she needed to fill Caleb in on the current problem. She'd just have to do the best she could with what had just happened and leave the past out of it. She took a deep breath preparing herself to tell the story. The bigger question was whether he'd believe her.

"All right. You have my full attention."

She nodded. Better to just get it over with and explain what happened. "I've been working as a personal chef for an Atlanta family for the last six months. Two nights ago was my night off, but I ran by the house to pick up some recipe notes I had left in the kitchen for a soufflé I wanted to try. While I was there, I heard an argument between a man I didn't know and my employer Doc Perry. The argument got heated. My boss said he wanted to stop some sort of business arrangement they had. He said he didn't want to accept a shipment. But I have no idea what type of shipment they were talking about. The man accused my boss of trying to take business away from his boss."

"And what happened?" he asked.

She clenched her fists as her nerves really kicked in. Once she told him this, there was no turning back. Could she trust this police chief she'd just met two days ago? She feared the answer was ultimately no, but she had no choice right now.

"It's okay, Annie. I'm here to help. But I need to understand what happened first."

Her heartbeat kicked up and the beeping on the monitor beside her bed sped up. "Then the man took out a gun and shot my boss in the head."

Caleb's eyes widened. "Are you sure?"

"Yes, I'll never forget what happened as long as I live. He died right there on the spot. It was a fatal blow."

"After your boss was shot, then what?"

"I screamed. I couldn't help it. I was so scared. The man I didn't recognize threatened me. He said if I told anyone what I had seen or if I went to the police that he'd hunt me down. Given what had just happened, I believed he would make good on his threat. I started running away and he yelled for me to stop. But I didn't stop. I knew that he'd kill me too. Then he ran after me and fired some shots as I was getting away."

"And you didn't go to the police?"

She shook her head. "I was so afraid after what the killer said. I just got in my car and drove for a bit. Thankfully, I had a duffle bag in my car with a few things that I hadn't unpacked from my last trip. Then when I saw the signs for Maxwell, I thought it would be a good idea to stop and figure out a game plan."

"Back up for a minute. Who is your boss, again?"

"His name is Doc Perry. He's a member of one of the most influential families in Atlanta. He's an admired businessman and very active in the community."

"And did the shooter say who he was working for?"

She nodded. "Yes. A man named Tim Silva."

"Are you absolutely sure that's what he said?" Caleb asked.

"Positive."

Caleb didn't say anything, but pulled out his phone and started typing while creasing his brow.

"You're scaring me, Caleb. What's going on?"

Caleb looked up. "Tim Silva runs one of the biggest organized crime syndicates in the southeast. If your boss was working with him, then he was involved with an extremely dangerous man."

"And the shooter?"

"Probably one of Silva's hired guns."

"How do you know so much about Silva?"

"He doesn't impact a lot of what goes on in Maxwell—at least not yet, thankfully. But he is very active in Atlanta."

"Wow. I had no idea."

"And what about last night? Who was the man who attacked you?"

"I went to go see Phil Perry. Phil is Doc's youngest son. He's the one who initially interviewed me for the job. We had a good working relationship, and I honestly thought he needed to be told about his father, and warned about the potential threat. To the best of my knowledge, Phil wasn't involved in Doc's family business. But I think I might have been wrong about that."

"What happened before he attacked you?"

"I told him what I had witnessed at Doc's house. He said I was never meant to be there. He apologized, but he said that I had a target on my back and that..."

"That what?"

"Silva would never let me live because I knew too much."

"Unfortunately, Phil was able to escape last night. My first priority was your safety. Did you tell Phil that you were staying in Maxwell?"

"No. I didn't bring that up. He'd have no way of knowing. No one would have reason to look for me there."

"That's good. Because I want to be able to take you back to Maxwell. It will be much safer there for you than in Atlanta."

"Thank you for that. So you believe what I'm telling you?" She held her breath as she waited to hear his response.

"Yes, I do. But I need to contact the FBI ASAP."

"Please. Are you sure that's the best course of action. I don't know who all is involved with Silva and what happened with Doc and Phil."

"Don't worry. This is someone I know I can trust."

"How can you be so sure?"

"Because he's my twin brother."

***

Caleb watched as Annie's eyes widened.

"You have a twin?" she asked.

"Yes. Not identical, but we are twins. Mac's an FBI agent, and he's done some work before on the Silva organized crime syndicate. We need to share this intel with him."

"Is he in Atlanta now?" she asked.

"No. He actually lives in Maxwell. He just moved back home this year. He goes into Atlanta a couple of days a week, and then works a lot of the cases outside the city. That allows him to live close to home."

"I'm putting my life into your hands right now, Caleb."

He looked at Annie. She looked fragile lying in the hospital bed. Her long brown hair tousled and the color having left her cheeks. He realized that she was right. If he messed this up, something could happen to her. But he refused to let that happen. "Don't worry, Annie. You have my word that I will protect you."

She didn't say anything in response, and he could see that she still had some doubt in her eyes. She was truly concerned for her safety. And he understood that. But it still felt like she was holding something back from him. That he was only hearing part of the story. "I'm giving you my word, and I'm a man of my word. You decided to let me in on your problem, so now let me do what I can. Okay?"

She nodded. "Thank you, Caleb." She paused. "And for what it's worth, I believe you."

The instant connection he had with this woman was undeniable. He didn't know where it was coming from, but he had a strong urge to protect her at all costs. *Lord, did you send Annie to Maxwell?*

But protection would be where it would stop. Caleb had long since given up on finding love. The wounds of war had made him wary of romantic relationships. He'd suffered enough pain and loss in his life.

He pulled out his phone and texted his brother that he needed to talk to him ASAP. "We'll see if he responds."

"I'm ready to get out of here." She looked around the hospital room.

"I don't blame you. The doctor should be coming by soon to discharge you."

"Then we'll go back to Maxwell, right? I didn't show up for work today. That doesn't look good."

"Don't worry. I already called in and covered for you."

"You did?"

"Yes. And they are fine. Missy is going to sub today."

"Can I still keep working at Pa's?"

"I'd actually prefer you to keep working at Pa's so you won't be alone. There's always customers around, and in addition to myself, I'll have officers do regular check-ins on you just to be on the safe side. But for now, things should be safe because Silva and his men have no reason to look for you there."

"Thank you. I need to keep myself busy or I'll go crazy. I can't stay cooped up all day and night by myself in the Inn."

"I've also sent an officer to your apartment this morning to gather more clothes and essentials for you. They didn't report any signs of suspicious activity when they were there. But I need to start a full investigation to figure out what the real threats are here." Now that he'd jumped into this, it was his mission to keep this woman safe.

CHAPTER THREE

Annie was relieved that Caleb hadn't stopped her from working the day shift at Pa's Diner. Two days had passed by quickly with no problems, and she had enjoyed staying busy during the day, and having the companionship of the diners.

But she also knew that Caleb had taken some security precautions. Each day a couple of different officers stopped by to check on her—even though they didn't say a word. She felt a mix of comfort and anxiety at their presence.

Even though she was doing okay in Maxwell, she knew this was far from over. Right now, she didn't see how it could end well. But she had to trust that Caleb would be able to protect her, even if that required her to go far outside her comfort zone.

It was mid-afternoon when Caleb walked into Pa's and sat down at the counter. She noticed it was the same spot he had sat in the other day. At that time of day there wasn't much going on, so she walked out of the kitchen to speak to him.

"Hi," she said.

"All going okay here?" he asked.

"Yes. Do you want something to eat?"

"No, thanks. I had something earlier during our staff meeting."

The front door to Pa's opened and Annie watched as a striking long haired brunette walked in. She wore a tailored black pantsuit with a lavender blouse. The woman made eye contact with her before making a direct path to Caleb and throwing her arms around him in a tight embrace.

This had to be Caleb's girlfriend. And she was stunning. But why did she care? It wasn't like she and Caleb had anything going on. He was doing his job. Nothing more.

"Annie," Caleb said as he put his arm around the brunette. "I'd like you to meet my baby sister, Gabby."

For a moment she didn't respond. Then she processed what Caleb had just said, and she felt like an idiot as she shook Gabby's hand. "Nice to meet you."

"You too." Gabby smiled at her, but she could see the questions in Gabby's piercing dark eyes.

"Gabby is a private investigator," Caleb said. "I thought she could help us."

She took in a breath. This was good news. "That's a great idea. We need someone who isn't on the inside of law enforcement." She much preferred someone on the outside although she wasn't going to tell them her other reasons for feeling that way right now.

"Caleb, if you don't mind, I'd like to talk to Annie alone for a few minutes," Gabby said.

Uh oh. Annie's antenna immediately went up.

"Sure. Annie, I'll be back when your shift is over to pick you up to take you to the Inn," he said.

He'd been escorting her to the Inn each evening. "Thank you." All a sudden, Annie hoped for an influx of customers, but that was highly unlikely at three in the afternoon.

"Why don't we have a seat and chat," Gabby said.

Annie forced a smile and sat down at the booth across from Gabby.

"So my brother filled me in on the situation."

Annie nodded. "Okay."

"But I still have some questions." Gabby leaned forward in her seat.

This all of a sudden didn't feel much like a chat and much more like an interrogation. She had flashbacks of her police interrogations in Florida after the shooting when she was only seventeen. Yes, she'd claimed self-defense and rightfully so. But the police had never acted like they had believed her. They'd accused her of wrongdoing—of telling lies—even though she had visible injuries. She tried to steady herself and focus on Gabby. "Sure. I'll answer whatever I can."

"You said that you went back to the Perry house the night of the murder because of a recipe?"

"Yes. I'd left some notes there for the dessert I was planning to do the next day and I wanted to pick them up to test it out. I like to try to perfect recipes before I serve them."

"There was no other reason?"

"No. I'm sorry, but I feel like I'm missing something."

Gabby cocked her head to the side. "It just seems strange that you'd want to go to work on your night off."

"Being a chef is a way of life for me. I'm constantly thinking about recipes and ideas. I'd been working on a complicated soufflé recipe, and I wanted to test some changes on my day off." She tried to keep her voice even, but she couldn't help being a bit annoyed about what Gabby seemed to be questioning.

"And you never heard anything before that night that seemed suspicious at the Perry household? Anything at all?"

"No. It was very much what you would expect." It didn't matter that this was Caleb's sister. She wasn't going to sit back and take the bullying. "I'm sorry, Gabby. But if you want to accuse me of something, please just come out and say it."

Gabby smiled which puzzled Annie even more.

"You've got a backbone. I like that," Gabby said. "And I'm sorry if you think my questioning is out of line. But the way I see it, I don't only have your safety in mind, but also that of my big brother."

"I wouldn't do anything to try to harm your brother."

"It would be very convenient if you were working with Silva. You could be one of his moles."

Annie couldn't help but laugh. "Yeah, because I'm so the type that would work for an organized crime boss. Just look at me. I'm a chef. I have no criminal abilities or desires for that matter. I live a very modest lifestyle. Feel free to verify that for yourself."

"So you think you were just at the wrong place at the wrong time?" Gabby asked.

"Yes, and now I appear to have a huge target on my back. You have to understand that I feel a bit ill equipped to handle that."

Gabby nodded. "I'm going to help you because my brother has asked me to, and I'd do almost anything for him. But let me make one thing abundantly clear. If I find out that you've been lying to Caleb—or to me—then there will be consequences. No one messes with my family."

She couldn't help but appreciate Gabby's fierce protective streak. Annie didn't have that in her own family. Growing up it was Annie always trying to protect her mom. Not the other way around. And now Annie was all alone in the world.

"I'm going to do some digging and see what I can figure out about Doc's connection to Silva and how Phil Perry comes into play."

"Isn't that dangerous?" Annie asked.

"Yes, but it's what I do. Don't worry. I live and operate under the radar."

"Is that why you're a PI instead of law enforcement? You like that better?"

"You're very perceptive, Annie."

A customer walked in and took a seat. Jen came out of the back to go take his order.

"Looks like you need to get back to work," Gabby said. "I'll be in touch. And be careful, Annie. These guys are dangerous."

Annie walked back to the kitchen as a wave of unease washed over her. It was clear that Gabby didn't trust her. But hopefully Gabby could find out information—information that might save her life.

For the next hour, Annie busied herself in the kitchen. Trying to keep her mind off of Silva and on cleaning up from her shift, she only had about an hour left to work when Jen walked into the kitchen. Jen stood a few inches taller than her, and she wore her long blonde hair pulled back in a low ponytail. Annie had instantly liked her.

"Can you hold down the fort for a minute?" Jen asked. "I need to run up to the store and pick up some cough medicine for Cindy."

"Sure. I don't think the dinner crowd will come in for a bit."

"Thank you. It's easier for me to pick it up before I get her from her after school program. I hope she's not coming down with something."

"Don't worry about it at all. I'll be fine here until you get back." Annie had a good idea of how hard it was to be a single mom because she had been raised by one.

Jen surprised her by grabbing her into a tight hug. "Thank you."

Jen left, leaving Annie to finish up her work. Annie could get used to having a friend like Jen. She couldn't remember the last time she had been hugged by anyone. It was part of her solitary lifestyle.

A couple of minutes later, she heard a sound behind her. "You're back super quick." Annie turned expecting to see Jen. But her heart skipped a beat when she saw the familiar blond muscle man who had murdered Doc.

She took a step back, but he caught her with a lunge forward. "It was a smart move to try to hide out in a town like this, Annie."

At the sound of him using her name, a chill shot down her arm. *Dear Lord, please save me from this man.* "How did you find me?" she asked. She had no connection to this town. That's why she thought it was safe to hide out in Maxwell.

"Your license was run by a police officer in this town. And I happen to have access into multiple law enforcement electronic systems."

"What do you want from me?" she asked. "I'm a nobody. I'm just a cook." Was there anyway she could talk him out of hurting her?

He smiled. "You don't expect me to believe that your presence at the Perry's was purely coincidental do you?"

"It w-was," she stuttered, hoping she could keep him talking.

But she also feared for Jen's life. The last thing she wanted to do was get Jen killed too. Jen had a little girl. Annie had to do everything in her power to stop this man. She had to think of a way out of this—and quick.

"I really am just a cook. I don't want to be involved in your business."

"Unfortunately for you, Mr. Silva doesn't feel that way. You were employed by a traitor. That's two strikes against you right there."

"I can't do anything to you. I don't even know who this Silva person is. I'd never even heard of him until the other night. Don't you understand that I have no interest in any of this? I'm not a part of that world, and I have no interest in becoming a part of it."

He took another step closing the gap between them. Her pulse kicked up even more.

"That isn't what Phil told me."

She let out a breath. "I didn't even think Phil was involved with his father's business. I'm telling you. I'm the one in the dark here, and I'm absolutely not a threat to anyone else."

He raised an eyebrow. "I have a job to do, and I can't take that chance."

Before she could take another breath, he wrapped his strong hands tightly around her neck and squeezed tightly, causing her vision to blur.

"I can make this quick. Or you can resist and it will be much more painful. Do you understand me?"

She nodded in response as she frantically tried to think about her options. She was absolutely no match for this man who appeared to be a trained killer. But she refused to just give up as she sent up another prayer.

As his grip tightened on her neck, she had a decision to make. Because if she didn't try to resist now, she'd be dead within the next minute.

With all the strength she could muster up, she picked up her right foot and slammed it down onto his left. Then she repeated the same move.

He grunted but he probably had at least a hundred pounds on her. There was no chance she could actually prevail in a fight with this man. She feared that he could break her neck with one swift movement.

"You shouldn't have done that," he said. He loosened his grip for a fraction of a second.

But it was enough time for her to break free and hop back grabbing a large knife from the counter. Feeling like a cornered animal, she jabbed the knife toward him when he approached her.

But he was too fast and strong and was able to get the knife away from her. He lifted his arm, ready to strike. She shrieked.

"Don't move!"

She looked up and saw Caleb behind the assailant—his gun drawn.

"Drop the knife and turn around slowly," Caleb commanded. "Very slowly."

Annie realized she was holding her breath and she let it out. She watched as the man dropped the knife.

"Good," Caleb said. "Now turn around with your hands up."

The man started to turn slowly as Caleb had directed. But then he reached into his jacket and before Annie could even process what was happening, the man pulled out a gun. But Caleb reacted even faster. A gunshot rang out as Annie crouched down by the counter. She peered up after a minute. She heard a groaning sound. The man was on the ground. Shot. But still alive.

She could hear Caleb calling in backup. Her entire body was shaking but she forced herself to keep it together. That had been way too close. *Thank you, Lord.*

"Annie, are you okay?" Caleb asked.

"Yes." But she was really far from it.

"Stay put until I can deal with him. The bullet just grazed him I think."

She took a seat in the corner of the kitchen and wrapped her arms tightly around her body. She realized she was probably in a bit of shock. The next few minutes went by in a blur as another officer arrived on the scene along with paramedics. Then Caleb came over to her.

"We need to get you checked out."

She shook her head. "I'm not really injured."

"By the look of the marks on your neck, I'd say otherwise."

She touched her neck and could feel the tender spots. But the thought of going to a hospital unsettled her. "Please," she said, "I don't want to go back to the hospital."

His eyes softened and he reached out and gently touched her shoulder. "Let the paramedics check you out. It won't take them long. And then you're going to stay at my place. I have plenty of extra space. I don't think it's safe for you to be alone at the Inn."

"Are you sure? I don't want to impose."

"You aren't imposing. Today showed that it's not safe for you to be by yourself."

She grabbed onto his arm. "Thank you. You just saved my life. Again."

***

"Here we are," Caleb said.

She took in a deep breath as he pulled the unmarked SUV up into his driveway. She couldn't believe she was going to be staying with a police officer. But Caleb had shown himself to be fiercely protective and loyal thus far and she had run out of options. They'd stopped by the Inn and picked up her stuff.

"This is your house?" Annie stared in awe up at the historic two-story home with the large front porch and tall white columns.

"Yes, it is. Gabby stays here sometimes when she's in town but she has her own apartment. She does a bit of traveling for her job. Your car is in the garage. One of my officers picked it up from the Inn and brought it here."

"Thank you. I hadn't even thought about that," she said.

"That's why I'm here."

"This is a big place."

"Tons of room for me plus other family who come and visit. And of course, my two dogs. I got a great deal on the place when the owner decided to retire down to Florida. I've loved this house since I was a kid, and knew one day if I could, I wanted to live here."

"It's amazing. So much character. Not like all the new construction."

"It has its benefits and disadvantages but overall I love it, and I have a nice big fenced-in yard in the back for the dogs." He ushered her up the front steps. She heard the sound of his dogs barking loudly with excitement.

He stopped outside the front door. "I hope you're okay with dogs."

She nodded. "I love dogs."

"Come on inside. I don't want to stand out here in the open."

She walked in and was greeted by two very excited balls of fur. One dog looked like a black lab and the other looked like a brown mix of some sort. But they were both large and very friendly.

"Down," Caleb said, his voice stern.

The dogs immediately obeyed him.

"And what are their names?"

"The black lab is Buddy and the brown mix is Bailey. I've only had them for about six months, but I've been really focused on their training. They were dropped off as strays at the station, and I just couldn't have them put down. That would've happened if I had taken them to the county shelter."

Annie was impressed with how composed the dogs were in the face of a new visitor. Their tails were wagging and tongues were hanging out of their mouths. But she was even more impressed with Caleb's big heart. "I love dogs. I don't mind if they get a bit excitable."

"Still, I don't like them jumping on people. Come on in, and I'll show you around."

They walked through the foyer into the living room with the dogs trailing close behind with wagging tails. The living room was spacious and held two big beige couches. She followed him into the bright and airy kitchen.

"I tried to tone down some of the colors from the previous owner, but it seemed right to keep the kitchen bright. I have a couple of spare bedrooms. You can take your pick."

"Thank you. Which one does Gabby use?"

"Top floor at the end of the hall on the left. All the others are up for grabs."

"Are you sure she won't mind?" She didn't think Gabby was thrilled about her when they met earlier, and now she was going to be staying here with Caleb.

"Gabby understands how serious the threats are against you. She will do everything she can to help. You don't have to worry about that."

She wasn't so sure about that, but she didn't push the issue. He gave her a few minutes alone to settle in. She couldn't believe she had taken refuge with the chief of police. It was the last place she would've thought to find safety, but there she was.

She chose a room on the second floor next to Gabby's at the opposite end of the hall from his. While he'd given her the option to stay on the first floor, he had said he would feel better with her being up there with him in case anything happened. She had a spacious room decorated in a beige and navy motif and her own private bath.

It was true that she would've preferred to stay at the Inn to have her independence, but right now really wasn't the time to focus on that. She was in danger. Silva wanted her dead, as evidenced by the attack today. And even though the shooter was in custody, Silva could just send someone else who would try to finish the job. So she didn't have any choice but to seek safety at Caleb's.

Lord, what were the Perry's involved with? She was certain that if it was worth killing over, it had to be quite a large illegal money making venture.

She took a few minutes to freshen up and examine the bruises that had formed on her neck. It could've been so much worse.

When she opened her bedroom door, she heard male voices coming from downstairs. Caleb had company and it definitely wasn't Gabby. For a minute her pulse kicked up. What if she couldn't trust Caleb? What if he was just like the police officer in charge she'd dealt with in Florida?

She walked slowly down the stairs and entered the kitchen to find a man talking to Caleb. She relaxed because she knew instantly that this had to be his twin. They shared the same build and facial structure. But Mac Winters's hair was almost black and his eyes were brown instead of blue.

"Annie," Caleb said. "This is my brother Mac."

She stretched her arm out to Mac to shake his hand.

"Sounds like you've had quite a roller coaster of events over the past few days. How are you holding up?" His eyes immediately honed in on her bruises.

"It's been challenging. First seeing my boss get murdered, then having Phil attack me, and now this." She paused. "But I just thank God that I'm alive. I don't even want to think about what would've happened to me if Caleb hadn't shown up at the diner today." She touched her neck reminding her of just how real it all had been.

Mac's dark eyes narrowed. "Unfortunately, the news I have from my end isn't going to be good."

"What's wrong?" she asked. Whatever Mac was about to say, Annie assumed the worst.

"I was just telling Caleb this when you came down." Mac looked at his brother and then back toward her. "You should have a seat."

She did as he said and sat down at the kitchen table. The men sat down too. She also noticed that Buddy the lab had decided to lie under her feet. She couldn't help but reach down and give Buddy a pat. "All right. Just give it to me straight. I can handle it."

"At the FBI, we've been working the Silva case for a while. But no matter how close we get, there's always been an issue with getting the evidence we needed against him to build a solid case. And now I think I've figured out the answer to that."

"And what is that?"

"I believe that Silva has someone on the inside at the FBI. I don't know who, but it explains why we get so close and then always manage to come up empty."

"What does this mean for me?"

Caleb looked at her. "Annie, normally in circumstances like this, where you had become a target of an organized crime group, you'd be taken to an FBI safe house. Especially until the threat was neutralized and a further security assessment conducted. But in this instance, it's not safe because we don't know who we can trust. Since the FBI may be compromised, they can't be brought into the equation. There's only one other FBI agent we could trust. But he's on his honeymoon right now. Which means, we're on our own for the next couple of days until he gets back."

"Caleb has volunteered to take on your personal security," Mac said. "You're safer here in Maxwell under Caleb's care, than anywhere else. Because as long as there is an insider working at the FBI, we can't go down the route of involving the Bureau. It's far too risky."

Caleb nodded. "This is the best security alternative right now. We can't trust the FBI. I'd much rather keep you here. I trust the officers I work with. And we have a couple of other backup options if needed. I've let my deputy chief know the situation. He is on board to assist."

"Okay," she said. Although she didn't automatically trust this deputy that she hadn't met. She was having a hard enough time relying on Caleb and his family.

"And we've got Silva's hit man in holding at the Maxwell jail," Caleb said. "He received medical care for his flesh wound which wasn't serious enough to put him in the hospital, so he's on lockdown. I'm going to interrogate him first thing in the morning and try to get as much information out of him as I can. Guys like him rarely turn on their bosses for fear of being killed. And we're in a tough situation because I'm not in a position to offer him any sort of immunity deal. I'll take a run at him and then decide who else we can involve."

"I'm sorry, Annie," Mac said. "It makes me sick to think the FBI could be compromised, but I'd be taking too much of a risk to assume otherwise. I haven't told anyone at the Bureau about you."

"And what about Phil? What if he goes to law enforcement and tells them I was at the house the night his father was killed?"

"He won't risk it," Caleb responded. "He needs to stay as far away from this thing as he can. If he tells them that you were there, that would lead to too many questions. But it is possible once the local PD gets into the investigation, that they will want to interview all the staff. Nothing we can do about that now though."

"I'll try to work my sources on the ground and see if there's any way I can run interference for you," Mac said. "But in the meantime for your own safety, you need to stay here with Caleb."

She nodded. "Believe me, guys, I get how dangerous this is. I'm not going to try to act like I can handle this all by myself. I'm a chef, not a police officer."

"Good." Mac stood up from the table. "I've got to get back to work. And once again, Annie, I'm sorry you're in this position."

"It's not your fault."

"I'll see you out," Caleb said.

Mac and Caleb spoke in hushed tones from the foyer. It was obvious to her that there was probably more to the complex web than they were telling her. But she had enough to handle with what she did know.

Caleb walked back into the kitchen. "Are you hungry?"

"Honestly, I don't think I could eat anything right now. I'm still a bit on edge from everything."

"That's totally understandable." He sat down across from her at the table.

Her mind was spinning, trying to determine how all of the pieces of the puzzle fit together. "You said earlier that the deputy chief here was on board. Who is he? Will I meet him?"

"His name is Mike Ramsey. He's actually been doing this a lot longer than I have. He's got about twenty years on me."

"Wow. You'll have to excuse me for asking, but isn't that strange that you're the chief then?"

He nodded. "It was a source of a bit of tension when I moved back home after I left the military. But when the former chief passed away of a heart attack, I was put in charge. Mike and I had a bit of a rough patch, but we're working together really well now. And between the two of us and my other officers, we're going to be on top of this."

"This Silva guy seems like a really dangerous and powerful man."

"Very. He isn't your run of the mill criminal. This is a highly complex organized crime syndicate. Silva has a wide network of people in a variety of different businesses working for him."

"Based on what I've told you, do you have any ideas about how Doc could've been involved?"

"The natural answer would be some type of drug trafficking. That's one of Silva's most lucrative businesses. Silva could've been using Doc's company to aid in his distribution. And beyond drugs, there could be other things too. Arms trafficking is a nasty business that Silva has a hand in too. And there are still quite a few more possibilities like money laundering. Maybe Doc realized that he could do some of the work on his own and cut out Silva. But that brings up the big question. He would need a source. Doc could have a masterful distribution plan and customers, but he has to have product to push."

"Seems like finding his source could be important to all of this. And there's something else that's bothering me too."

"What's that?"

"I didn't think Phil actively worked with Doc's company. It was actually a source of tension in the family. Phil was the only one in the family who did his own thing. He went out on his own and started a company. So how did he get involved?"

"I have no clue. We have more question marks than we do answers." He paused. "And we're not going to crack this case tonight. You should try to get some rest. You've been through a lot."

And there was one more thing that was bothering her. The secret of her past that she was keeping from Caleb. Because once he found it out, would he still trust her?

CHAPTER FOUR

Caleb looked into the eyes of Russ McCoy—the man who had attacked Annie and killed Doc Perry. He would eventually charge him with the murder of Doc Perry, but for now he had plenty of other crimes to charge him with and hold him in confinement in the Maxwell jail.

The first order of business was finding out how much McCoy had told to the others in the Silva network about Annie, because that would impact Caleb's entire security plan for Annie.

"Mr. McCoy, this will all go much easier for you if we play straight with each other. I don't have time for games and I don't think you want to try them with me."

McCoy looked at him, with no sign of concern on his face. "I don't have anything to say to you."

"Oh, I think you do. Or else I'll make sure Silva and all of his hired hands think that you told the police everything. That you sang like a bird."

McCoy frowned. "They would never believe that about me."

"If you want to go down that path, then try me. But I'll put in a good word with the DA that you cooperated when this is all over if, and only if, you tell me everything you know about Annie and what you've told others in the Silva organization about her."

McCoy leaned forward. "This is all about the girl, huh? Who is she to you?"

Caleb used all of his years of military training to keep his temper in check. McCoy was a professional. He wasn't going to crack easily. "Ms. Thomas is an innocent bystander in this situation."

McCoy rubbed his chin. "I don't specifically have a problem with her. But Silva knows who she is and what she claims to have seen. And he does have a huge problem with her."

McCoy knew better than to admit to the chief of police that Annie had seen him murder Doc. "Does anyone else in the Silva organization know that Annie is here in Maxwell?"

McCoy didn't immediately answer.

"Work with me here, McCoy."

"This is all you're going to get from me. I'm the only one who knows where she is. Silva thought she was still in Atlanta. I did some digging using my resources and saw that you had run her license. So I came to check out the neighborhood."

It bothered him that this criminal had a way to breach into the system, but for now he had to focus on the immediate threat. "And why should I take what you're telling me now at face value?"

"Because you're smart enough to realize that there are things I can tell you and things I absolutely won't. This woman had no business getting involved. But now that she is, all I can tell you is that Silva has a very long memory. Once she's on his list, it will be difficult to get her off of it."

"But not impossible," Caleb said, more to himself than to McCoy. "If I find out that you're lying to me about any of this, I will make your life much more difficult with the DA."

McCoy crossed his arms. "I've said what I'm going to say. I think we're done here."

They'd only just begun in Caleb's mind. "I don't know why you're in such a rush. You're not going anywhere." And neither was Caleb. He'd had to conduct interrogations as part of his special ops work. So this guy had no idea who he was dealing with.

"You can ask whatever you want. Doesn't mean I'm going to answer."

"Are you military?" Caleb couldn't help but ask.

"No. But I've done some for-hire work abroad."

That meant mercenary. This guy was even more dangerous than Caleb had originally thought. He had to keep him locked up and far away from Annie. "How long have you been working for Silva?"

"You know I'm not going to answer anything like that about Silva."

Caleb spent another hour trying to get McCoy to talk, but it was of no use. He had meant it when he said he wasn't going to talk about anything other than Annie. The only upside was that after spending time with the man, Caleb felt pretty certain that he was telling the truth about Annie. McCoy was the only one in the Silva network that knew she was staying in Maxwell. That was a critical piece of information that Caleb planned to factor into his strategy for keeping Annie safe.

He made sure McCoy was secure back in his cell and then walked out of the police station. He pulled out his cell and called Mac. He quickly recapped what had happened during the interrogation.

"So are you going to stay put here in Maxwell?" Mac asked.

"I know you can only trust a criminal so much, but I think McCoy was telling the truth. He seems more like a lone wolf. Out doing his own thing—largely shaped by his time as a mercenary."

"It's risky either way. At least staying here, you're on home turf. You've got your family to back you up. Plus the police force."

"Yeah, and I'm not at the point where I'm just going to up and leave. I know Mike could handle the police work, but I still think it's better to wait it out a bit. Get more information."

"I wish that Gabe were here," Mac said. "He has even more experience with Silva than I do, and would have some good ideas on this. Especially since we have a possible issue with one of our own in the FBI. But the last thing I'm going to do is bother him the last few days of his honeymoon. He and Hope don't deserve to have their trip ruined because of our problems here."

"You're right. Don't bother him. We can handle this. At least for now, anyway."

"Speaking of that. Are you sure you're comfortable with Gabby working on this case?"

"I hear you, bro. But Gabby has a mind of her own. We could try to get her to stop and that would only make her more convinced. I've warned her how dangerous Silva is. I think she gets the message. She's been in the trenches before."

"Doesn't mean we have to like it," Mac said. "She'll always be our baby sister."

"And right now she's at the house keeping watch over Annie."

"We need to get to bottom of this before someone else gets hurt...or even worse."

"I know." He could only pray that they could protect the innocent.

* * *

Annie was starting to go stir crazy, and it didn't help that Gabby's dark eyes were locked onto her like a laser beam. They sat in the living room with the TV on, but it was evident that Gabby wasn't watching it. Buddy was her new best friend and curled up beside her, while Bailey was lounging near where Gabby sat.

"I think you can relax a little bit, Gabby," Annie said. She made another attempt to put Gabby at ease, but the tension was mounting in the room.

Gabby gave the slightest of smiles. "It's not my job to be comfortable. It's my job to keep you safe. And that's what I intend to do."

"I highly doubt we have anything to worry about here at your brother's house. I think maybe you can take it down a notch."

Gabby shook her head. "That's exactly the type of thinking that can get you killed."

Annie sucked in a breath after hearing Gabby's blunt warning. "I'm not trying to be reckless."

Gabby sighed. "Look. I know this is all a lot for you. You're not in law enforcement. Caleb told me you don't have experience with firearms either and only know basic self defense. So that's why I am here."

That was only the partial picture. The one experience with guns she did have turned out to be awful. Thoughts of pulling the trigger flooded through her mind.

Gabby kept on talking. "So you need to rely on the professionals to keep you out of harm's way."

Annie nodded. "Are you always like this?" she asked before she realized how it sounded.

"Like what?"

"Always so serious."

Gabby actually laughed. "I'm on the job right now. So I'm going to be focused on that. But I don't work twenty four seven every day of the year. Be glad that I'm not taking this lightly. My brother told me to keep watch, and that's what I'm going to do." Gabby looked at her watch. "Caleb should be home any minute, though. Maybe that will make you feel better."

"I don't mean to sound ungrateful. I'm thankful for all of your help." Annie wanted to ask more questions to get to know Gabby but figured it was better not to push things.

She took a moment to pat Buddy's head, and he looked up at her with his soulful dark eyes. Her heart melted. She'd never been able to have any pets growing up, and she'd always begged her mom for a dog. But in retrospect she understood that her mother was a complete mess and wasn't even able to take care of her—much less an innocent animal. She pushed back the thought that one day she could have her own dog and a normal well-adjusted family. Because that just wasn't going to happen.

Her thoughts were interrupted by a loud knock on the door.

Gabby jumped up from the navy armchair with her gun drawn. "Stay put. I'll check the door."

Her heartbeat started thumping wildly. What if Gabby was right? What if they weren't safe at Caleb's house? What if there was an army of Silva's men right outside waiting to kill them both.

Gabby looked through the peephole of the front door. "Who's there?" she asked.

It obviously wasn't someone she knew.

"It's Phil Perry."

At the sound of his voice, fear gripped her again. Phil had come looking for her.

"I need to find Annie Thomas. It's very important," Phil said in a strained voice.

"About what?" Gabby asked.

"I want to help. I don't want to hurt her. I promise. I'm here with information. I'm in trouble, too."

Annie shook her head and made eye contact with Gabby pleading with her not to open the door. But it appeared Gabby had other ideas. She pulled out her phone and sent a message. Annie presumed it was to her brothers.

"Show me your hands. High. If you make any sudden moves, I will shoot. I'm armed."

Gabby slowly opened the door and motioned for Phil to come in. But she had the gun pointed directly at his head. One false move and Annie was certain that Gabby would make good on her threat.

But when Phil walked in, he looked to be anything but a threat. His shirt was untucked and had blood stains on it. His hair was disheveled and he had a large purple bruise on his left check.

He looked over at her with bloodshot eyes. "I'm so sorry, Annie. I'm in way over my head."

"You tried to kill me, Phil."

The door was still open and Caleb walked in. When he saw what was happening, he pulled out his gun.

"It's okay, Caleb," Gabby said.

"What in the world is going on here?" Caleb's blue eyes were questioning Gabby, but then he looked at Annie. Then at Phil. Keeping his gun trained on Phil with his right hand, he used his left to take out his handcuffs. Phil didn't put up a fight.

"You can cuff me. I need your help. I'm not a threat to you. Do whatever it is you need to do."

"Phil Perry, you're under arrest." Caleb proceeded to read Phil his rights.

Annie couldn't believe what was happening. She watched as Caleb took Phil into the kitchen and sat him down at the table. Phil was completely compliant. And he didn't look like the confident, outgoing man she'd come to know. He looked more like a wounded animal.

Gabby and Caleb were talking, but Annie realized that she'd been in a haze watching the scene unfold. She'd followed them as they went, but then she took a few steps closer until Caleb lifted his hand in a stop motion.

"That's close enough," he told her. "Please sit down at that end of the table."

She wanted to argue since it was clear that Phil wasn't currently a threat to her. But she didn't.

"I'm going to check outside to just be sure the area is secure and then do some recon. I'll check back in later. You have this situation under control." Gabby said. Then she walked out leaving her and Caleb with Phil.

"Start talking," Caleb said.

But instead of Phil looking at Caleb, he directed his attention back toward her. "Annie, again, I'm so sorry. I know what I did was unforgivable, but this whole situation has gotten out of control. I'm a coward."

"Phil, the best thing you can do now to help me is to answer Caleb's questions. He's the chief of police here in Maxwell."

Phil nodded. "I don't even know where to begin, though."

Caleb sat down across from Phil. "Let's start with what you know about your father's relationship with Silva."

Annie waited as Phil took a few deep breaths. Even though this man had tried to kill her, she felt sorry for him.

"My father met Silva through a mutual acquaintance a couple of years ago at a charity event in Atlanta. At that time, my father had no interest in Silva's business."

"Which is?" Annie jumped in and asked.

"Silva's network is extensive. Drug trafficking is his primary business but he had his hands involved in money laundering, gun running and I don't even know what else. Plus it expands all throughout the southeast. He has a business partner who runs part of the region and then his cousin runs the Florida operations. I know they have a complex drug network in south Florida."

A chill shot down her back. Annie was all too familiar with the dark side of life in south Florida where she had grown up. Her mom bouncing from random apartment and even more random men. And most of the men were involved in some sort of drugs or other criminal activity.

"What changed to make your father want to get involved?" Caleb asked.

"My father started to have more time on his hands. He'd largely turned over day to day operations of his investment firm to my two older brothers. I have a percentage of the company but no managing control at this point." Phil slumped down in the chair. "Looking back maybe that was part of the problem. Part of why I turned on him, because he had excluded me. But back to your question. My father started doing side investments. Some gambling and other things. And I think he thought investing in Silva's business would be fun. He'd live on the edge a bit and make a stellar return."

"Because of the illegal nature of the business, he stood to make more money," Caleb said flatly.

"Exactly. And there was the thrill of operating outside of the law that I think was attractive to him. My father was so rich and powerful he thought that he was above the law and could do pretty much whatever he wanted. It started with my father making investments. But then about six months ago, he and Silva became closer. My father wanted to understand more of the business. And at that point, Silva trusted him. But my father was too smart for his own good. He tried to cozy up to some of the players and suppliers and siphon off business for himself. Cutting Silva out of the equation."

"And when Silva started sniffing around, that's when he came to me." Phil looked at her again. "I realize all of this in hindsight. I was such a fool. If I would've kept my big mouth shut, maybe none of this would've happened. Maybe my father would still be alive right now."

"What did you do?" she asked.

"Like I said. I was upset that my father chose my two brothers over me. I was basically third in line to run the business. And given our ages, there's no way that I would've ever been a major player in father's investment business. Yes, I have some percentage ownership which means I get a part of the profits, but only a fraction of what my brothers get."

"Silva used you," Caleb said.

"Yes. He knew my father's weak points. He knew my weak points. And he capitalized on them. He came to me with what I thought was an amazing offer. But now I can see that he totally tricked me."

"How so?" Caleb asked.

"He made up a story about some new business venture he had with my father and how he wanted to bring me in, but that he needed some information on my father's current contacts. When I gave him the names of those my father was dealing with, I think it confirmed to Silva that my father was going to cut him out. And when I finally figured out what was going on, it was too late. The damage had already been done and there was no going back."

"How did you find out about your father's death?" Caleb leaned forward in his chair.

"My older brother found him. When I heard of the suspicious circumstances, I knew right away. I met with one of Silva's men who told me about how things would play out. They were still willing to work with me as long as I did my best to get rid of you, Annie. That's a loose end they didn't want to have hanging out there."

"But now you think they've changed their minds?" Annie asked.

"Yes. I was roughed up by one of his guys after you got away from me. Then last night I was run off the road. I don't believe it was an accident. They're going to try to kill me too. I obviously know too much. I was a greedy idiot for thinking I could come out of this on top."

"And now you're in trouble." Annie didn't want anything to happen to Phil. But she didn't know how Caleb would handle all of this.

"He is in trouble, but you'll be safe in a guarded cell in the Maxwell jail."

Phil nodded. "I figured you'd want to lock me up. But don't you think I'd be more valuable to you on the outside?"

Caleb shook his head. "Even putting aside the fact that I'm charging you with attempted murder and assault, it's for your own good. You already said that Silva is after you. That's the only way I can guarantee your safety."

"All right. And there are a couple of other things I need to tell you."

"What?" Caleb asked.

"Silva has a source inside law enforcement. I don't know who it is, but I know he gives Silva intel and that Silva relies on him."

Annie watched as Caleb's expression remained unchanged. But she already knew about the suspicions Caleb and Mac had about a mole inside the FBI. This solidified that theory.

"And you don't have any further information on his identity?" Caleb narrowed his eyes at Phil.

"No. Just that he's law enforcement."

"And what else did you want to tell us?"

Phil looked at her and then back to Caleb. "There's been talk about Silva expanding out to some of the smaller towns to handle some of his operations. And Maxwell was on the list."

"Are you sure?" Caleb's voice came out raspy.

Annie knew that this bit of information had taken Caleb off guard.

"I can't say that I know it's happening, just what I've heard from some of my contacts."

"Okay. I'm going to escort you to the station. Annie, I'll call in another officer to stay here with you while I'm gone."

"No," she said quickly, before she even realized it.

Caleb looked over at her, confusion in his blue eyes. "Are you all right, Annie?"

"I'd just prefer it if you stayed here and got another officer to escort Phil."

"Sure." He looked at her. "That can be arranged. I'll call my deputy Mike now."

Annie didn't trust being alone with any other officer right now. The stakes were too high, and she'd been betrayed before.

***

Later that night Caleb sat on the couch beside Annie with Buddy curled up between them. She was stuck in the complicated and highly dangerous maze, and it was up to him to ensure her safety. Annie was an innocent woman caught in the crossfire. She didn't deserve any of this. Caleb had seen enough in his career in law enforcement to realize just how dangerous organized crime networks were.

He realized that he was starting to care more about Annie than he should, which didn't make any sense to him. Normally, he had no problem building up a wall around him when it came to women. It was his MO. But Annie seemed to shake up his entire viewpoint without even trying. She didn't even appear to understand that she was having any impact on him.

But there was something else going on with her. She'd had a visceral reaction when he'd told her he was going to leave her with another officer while he escorted Phil to holding. She hadn't had any issue staying with Gabby. He didn't want to push her into the conversation, but he also needed to understand where she was coming from. Was there a part of all of this that she had kept hidden? He needed to know.

"Annie." He looked over at her. "How are you holding up?" First he needed to see how she was doing. Most people wouldn't have been able to handle even a part of what she'd lived through the past couple of days.

"Better than Phil," she said flatly.

"You're a strong person. I can see it in your eyes and how you've handled yourself. On the other hand, Phil has probably been used to having it easy his whole life." He paused, thinking about the best way to start this topic of conversation with her. "But there's something else going on with you, Annie." He wanted to provide her with a chance to explain what was bothering her—besides the obvious.

"Caleb, I really can't thank you enough for what you've done for me. Stepping into a dangerous situation when you didn't have to. You've saved my life and been next to me each step of the way through this terrible ordeal."

"You can tell me. Whatever it is, I'm sure I'll understand." He wanted her to know that she could be open and frank with him.

She broke eye contact with him. "I'm not so sure about that."

"Give it a try."

"I don't have faith that other police officers would treat me the same way that you do."

"And why is that?"

"If I tell you why, then it will probably change how you see me. And not for the better."

He had no idea where she was going with this. "Why don't you let me be the judge of that?"

She nodded. "Before I begin, I need to tell you a bit about my past, if that's all right?"

"Sure. I want to hear all about it." And that was true. He wanted to know more about this woman.

"I had a very rough childhood. My mom was a complete train wreck. She had an awful track record with the wrong men. I never even knew my dad. We didn't live anywhere long and they were all pretty bad places in totally sketchy neighborhoods. I was often left alone between my mom working and then out partying."

"I'm so sorry."

"Yeah, after having met your two siblings, I can tell you that I had nothing even coming close to resembling that type of family. The way the three of you have each other's backs, the love and loyalty that is there, is a totally foreign concept to me. It was just me and my mom, and most often, I was more like the parent than the child. She'd go off on binges and it was up to me to provide for myself. To get myself to and from school. To try to focus on doing well, even when there was so much strife back at home. Because when she was around it was usually to bring home a guy."

"Where is your mom now?"

Annie's eyes misted over, and he immediately knew the answer before she responded.

"Her lifestyle caught up with her. She died of a drug overdose a few years ago. I can't even say that I was surprised. I had tried to break through to her, but nothing ever stuck. She grew up in a troubled environment. That was all she knew."

Caleb couldn't help himself as he reached out and grabbed onto her hand. "I'm so sorry, Annie." Saying he was sorry seemed like such an inadequate response, but that was all he could say.

"She had so many issues and personal demons. She always told me that I wasn't like her, that I was meant to be able to get out of the vicious cycle that she had lived her entire life, and that I could be something more one day. It's one of the things that motivated me to become a trained chef. I wanted to be independent and secure. To know that I could stand on my own two feet, and not seek out help from others." She paused. "But none of that explains my hesitancy about the officer earlier."

"If you don't want to talk about it now, I understand." She'd already opened up some pretty deep wounds. He knew how hard it was to talk about these things.

"No, it's better this way. Just to get it all out there right now. Like I said, my mom picked the wrong type of men. Not just guys that weren't a perfect match. I'm talking about men who were involved in drugs and worse. Guys you did not want to cross. The guys she dated did have money, but it was dirty money. My mom flitted from one bad guy to the next. I don't ever remember her dating normal guys. I tried to shield myself from it the best I could. But then one day it all caught up to me."

"What happened?" A million awful thoughts ran through his mind.

"I was seventeen and was just about to finish up my senior year in high school. I was at home in the apartment by myself. And my mom had given her boyfriend a key. From the moment he stepped inside the front door, I knew he was strung out on drugs and had been drinking. He demanded to know where my mom was. She hadn't gotten off her shift at work yet. Then he started to go on a rampage. He roughed me up a bit. I tried my best to fight him off. Then he started throwing things around the kitchen. While he was trashing the kitchen, I ran to my mom's room and grabbed her gun out of the nightstand. I'd never used a gun before, but I was so afraid. He was so full of rage." She paused and took another breath. "He'd already hurt me. I thought he might kill me. I was just a child. I shut the door to my mom's room and locked myself in."

Caleb clenched his fists as his anger at this man grew with each word that came out of Annie's mouth.

"After a few minutes, he busted down the door and came toward me. I told him to stop and he didn't. That's when I shot him in the leg."

"You had every right to defend yourself, Annie."

"That's what I thought, too. And I didn't try to kill him. I was no gun expert, but I tried to aim for his leg thinking that would be better than anything else. I was just trying to stop him from hurting me. That's all I was trying to do."

"What happened to him?"

"He survived. He lost a bit of blood but there was a lasting effect—he walks with a severe limp because of me."

"And the police?" He hated to ask. He was starting to put the pieces together, and he had a pretty good idea where this was going.

"I thought they would be on my side. Up to that point in my life, I assumed that police helped the innocent. I was a young girl being attacked by a criminal. But they took his side. I underwent hours of interrogation. They tried to get me to change my story. Tried to get me to say that I was the aggressor. They didn't buy my self-defense claim."

"Did they charge you?"

"No. Thankfully, in the end, another detective was brought onto the case, and he believed me enough to keep the charges from sticking."

"Dirty cops," Caleb muttered to himself.

"Exactly. My mom's boyfriend had friends who had some pretty important criminal connections. Looking back it's all so clear now. But at the time, as a seventeen year old girl, my life felt like it was falling apart. I didn't understand why they didn't believe me." She sucked in a breath. "I was telling the truth."

"I believe you."

"You do? Just like that?"

"I know we haven't known each other that long, but I can see you're telling me the truth."

"So you can see why, even though I realize there's no connection to those police in Florida and the ones here, I don't know that I'll ever get over that. It's one of the reasons I left Florida. I wanted to get away from that man. I feared he would come after me again, given what I did to him, because he is permanently injured. He's not the type of man to forget and move on."

"Did he threaten you?"

"Yes, multiple times. But soon after that day, I graduated and turned eighteen. I left the state. I went to culinary school, and I had no intention to ever go back there again. Especially after my mom's death."

"Do you still think he's looking for you?"

"It's not a risk I'm willing to take. He's a really bad guy."

"But you acted in self defense."

"I know that, but he didn't exactly see it that way. He was so strung out, he didn't remember everything. That's why he was able to spin this totally separate story to the cops. He concocted a pure fiction that I had been the one drinking and he had tried to get me under control and stop me. And that's why I shot him." She paused. "I could work at larger restaurants and have been scouted a few times, but it's not worth the risk. So that's one of the reasons I prefer to work as a private chef."

"You want to make sure that he won't ever be able to track you down. If you were ever in the limelight because of your work in a restaurant, then you fear that he could get to you?"

She nodded. "See, I told you I was a mess."

"You shouldn't have to limit your career options because of this criminal."

The longer Annie talked about this man, the more upset Caleb became. This guy had thrown her entire life off track.

"Maybe we should worry about one problem at a time. Right now Silva is my problem. But you get a better picture of my past and my hang-ups when it comes to law enforcement."

"What happened to you is awful. But I promise you that most police officers are honest." And he believed that with all of his heart. He worked with so many noble and loyal officers.

"And I know that from a logical standpoint, but it still makes trusting very hard. Even trusting you. But you've not given me any choice." She gave him a faint smile.

"I'm not going to let you down, Annie. That I promise you."
And he meant every word.

Annie wasn't the only one with nightmares from the past.
Listening to hers only lifted his more to the surface. The fact that
he'd let down his friend in Afghanistan when his SEAL teammate had needed him the most. But there was no way he was
going to let history repeat itself with Annie.

* * *

Caleb lay in his bed, but sleep just wasn't happening. His mind
was working overtime. He had committed to protect Annie, but
there were many more questions than answers. Her story about
what had happened in Florida sickened him. He became a police
officer to serve and protect. After his time in the military and
being a Navy SEAL, he knew he still wanted to do something
for the greater good. And that's why he'd chosen to go into law
enforcement. Serving a greater purpose was part of his DNA.

That those police in Florida were in criminals' back pockets instead of protecting an innocent seventeen year old girl was
unfathomable to him. It was amazing that Annie was so resilient.
Given all she had been through, a lot of people would've never
been able to live productive lives. Between her difficult upbringing with her mom and then having to defend herself like that
against a violent man. And who knows how many other horror
stories she probably had relating to her time growing up.

He knew he had a problem with trying to fix people. His urge
to help fix people and their problems came naturally, but was
only compounded by what had happened in the war—when he
tried his hardest and couldn't help the teammate who needed
him the most.

But in this instance, he wasn't trying to fix Annie. She was
perfect just the way she was. He did feel a fierce need to protect her

though. And the fact that he was having those types of thoughts scared him. He was developing feelings for this woman, and that was something he simply hadn't allowed himself to do in years.

Why her out of all the women in the world? A woman who couldn't stand people in law enforcement—and rightfully so, after what she'd been subjected to.

To be able to keep Annie safe he needed to understand all the threats that she faced. His police instincts just told him that there was something more going on with the Silva situation. But he didn't know what he was missing. It bothered him that something still seemed off. Generally, his instincts regarding his investigations were spot on. But there was this nagging feeling that made him think he had to dig deeper. He was missing something.

A loud piercing scream had him shooting up out of the bed, grabbing his gun from his nightstand, and running down the hallway to Annie's room. He prayed that he wouldn't be too late.

He pushed opened the door, flipped on the light, his gun drawn and ready to take out the perpetrator, his heart beating rapidly. But the room was empty except for Annie who was sitting up in the bed with the purple blanket wrapped tightly around her.

"Annie," he said. "Are you all right?"

"Yes, I'm sorry to wake you. I guess I was just having an awful nightmare. It was so bad it woke me up."

He let out a huge sigh of relief and walked closer to the bed. Nightmares he could handle. Buddy and Bailey also joined them in the room, and Buddy jumped up on the bed with Annie. He'd noticed that his lab had fallen in love with her.

"Sorry, Annie. Buddy, get down," he commanded.

"No," she said quickly. "Please let him stay up here with me and keep me company."

It warmed his heart that Annie apparently had the same love of dogs that he did. "Is there anything I can get you? Maybe some water?"

She shook her head. "No. I'll be fine. I'm sorry to have woken you."

He watched as she stroked Buddy's back. Buddy looked perfectly content with Annie by his side. "Don't apologize. You've experienced a lot over the past few days. It's totally natural that you'd have nightmares."

"Thanks. I think it's all starting to catch up to me. Especially after we talked about my past earlier. It's common for me to have nightmares when that is on my mind. It's not something I have ever really discussed with anyone. As you can imagine, it's a difficult subject to bring up. No one wants to admit that they shot someone and were then wrongfully accused."

"But remember that you weren't in the wrong." He thought for a moment. "Do you want to talk for a bit?" He actually wanted her to say yes. Maybe it was him who needed to talk.

"I'll be fine here with my canine bodyguard." She patted Buddy on the head. "I don't want to interrupt your sleep any more than I have."

He shook his head. "You aren't interrupting anything."

"You must think I'm a total disaster."

He shook his head. "Not at all. I think you're going through a really rough patch right now. And if you were unfazed by all of this, I'd think there was something wrong with you."

"Times like this really push me to rely on my faith in the Lord."

"I can totally relate to that feeling." Knowing that they shared the same faith only made him more drawn to her.

"I know God has a plan, but sometimes it's not clear to me what it is or how it's going to work out."

"God is always in control. Even when it seems like He's not." Since she'd opened up to him, he thought he should do the same with her. At least a little bit. "I will tell you there were some dark times I faced when I was deployed. Some of the things I witnessed and endured. And there were some points when I wondered how God could let something so awful happen." He paused for a moment to collect himself. He wasn't going to talk about everything that he had experienced during the war in the mountains of Afghanistan, while chasing down terrorists. It was too hard to speak to anyone about.

"I can't even begin to comprehend what you went through when you were deployed."

He shook his head. "I wasn't telling you this to get your sympathy, but to let you know that I have issues, too. You're not alone in that, Annie. It's just that sometimes our baggage takes different forms"

"But you're so strong."

"It maybe appear that way now, but I've gone through some rough spots. Times when I was caught up in my own fear instead of turning it all over to God. When I came back from my last deployment three years ago, I was in a dark place."

"How did you get through it?"

He barely did. But he was trying to be more optimistic right now to help her see that there was a path out of this situation. The last thing he wanted to do was to bring her down. "When I realized that the only way I found courage was through faith in God, I regained peace. It was a slow process of building my faith in the context of everything I'd gone through. But that process made me much closer to God and forced me to rely on Him. Because when I was trying to shoulder it all by myself, I was failing miserably."

"That's powerful to hear how God has worked through your life in such a profound way. I probably wouldn't even be here today if it wasn't for my faith. My mom had a lot of flaws, but the one thing she did do is make sure I went to church. I'd often go by myself because she couldn't or wouldn't go. But she insisted that I needed to. She said that it would help lead me down a different path than her. I didn't get it when I was young, but as I grew older and stronger in my faith, I understood. So I'm thankful that in that one most important area, she got it right."

"Yes, she did."

"Thanks for listening."

"With His help we're going to get through all of this."

CHAPTER FIVE

The next two days went by slowly. Gabby hovered over Annie like a mama lion during the day while Caleb was working. Annie was always relieved when Caleb came home because he gave her more space than his sister. Gabby's constant state of high alert was starting to make Annie incredibly anxious. She was appreciative that Gabby cared so much, but it was all taking its toll on her.

Even though she'd spent a lot of time with Gabby, she wasn't really getting to know her. Gabby was all business, so that mostly left Annie to her own thoughts.

Annie still couldn't believe that she had opened up to Caleb. Even now at twenty-eight years old, the events of her past gripped onto her heart threatening to squeeze it into pieces. This wasn't about what was the most logical or rational—it was about her deep seeded fears.

Sometimes she felt herself recede into that seventeen year old girl who had been betrayed by those who were supposed to protect her. And that didn't even begin to touch the surface on all of the unresolved issues she had because of her mother. There was no doubt in her mind that she was damaged. That's why it was so much easier to not let anyone get close. When she was cooking she wasn't living in the past and could focus on her true passion—food.

She'd stayed away from romantic relationships because she had a distrust of men. She wasn't willing to take the plunge on a guy because she feared that she'd turn out just like her mother—codependent and struggling. It occurred to Annie that she had never seen her mother truly happy. Even with the various men in her life, she was lonely and miserable. Annie wouldn't live like that.

She sat at the kitchen table with a cup of tea and her now trusty sidekick Buddy close by. She had to admit that she had started to form an attachment to him. Something she specifically did not want to allow herself to do. But as he looked up at her with those big, kind brown eyes, how could she not feel a connection with the pup? And she had a strong feeling that, unlike humans, Buddy wouldn't ever let her down. Caleb and Gabby had just made the security handoff. And she was glad she could relax a little now that Caleb was home.

Caleb walked into the kitchen carrying grocery bags and smiled when he made eye contact with her.

"How was your day?" He set the bags down on the counter.

"Fine," she responded quickly.

"That doesn't sound like everything is fine."

"We need to talk about things. I can't just stay locked up here in your house day in and day out under Gabby's protective detail. I know she means well, but it only makes me more nervous. And I can't do anything I would normally do." She hadn't intended to unload on him, but once she'd started, it all came pouring out.

He nodded. "I realize that this isn't a long term solution to our problems."

"Isn't it really my problem, not yours?" She realized she was pushing him away, but she couldn't help it.

He walked over to where she sat and gently placed his hand on her shoulder. "No. It's my problem, too. This is my town. And even if it wasn't my town, I care about you, Annie."

Hearing his words touched her, but it also made her a bit worried. She wanted to believe that all of his intentions were good, but what if she were wrong?

"You're thinking something," he said.

"It's nothing." She couldn't say that she was confused about how she felt about him.

"Are you hungry? I bought some steaks. I thought we could grill on the back porch. At least that way you're getting some time outside."

"I have to tell you that grilling is not my area of expertise. I'm much better with a stove or oven." Yeah, she could throw steaks on a grill, but she held herself to such a high culinary standard.

"Well, it just so happens that I am a grilling expert. In fact, grilling is about the only thing I can do when it comes to cooking. But I do it very well if I do say so myself." He laughed. "So just sit back on the porch and relax with the dogs. I'll do all the work. It's a marvelous early spring day out there. Not too hot and humid yet."

She agreed because she wanted to have the time outside.

Later, she had cleaned her plate and settled into a chair on the back porch. The dogs had worn themselves out playing with their ball and Frisbee in the yard, and she let them back inside to rest and get some water. Caleb, true to his word, had been right at home in front of the grill.

He leaned forward in his chair. "So, be honest. I know you're the professional chef. How did I do on the steaks?"

She smiled. "It was delicious."

"And you're not just saying that to be polite?" he asked with a raised eyebrow.

She laughed. "No. I can't hide my feelings about food. I'm known to be a tough critic. And the fact that I ate all of it should tell you something."

"It's nice to hear you laugh."

"We haven't had much of an opportunity for things to laugh at."

"I know. But remember you aren't going through this alone, Annie. I'm right here."

"I know."

As she looked into his blue eyes, she felt a yearning for a deeper connection with him. But it was foolish to think that she would ever be able to open her heart to a man—especially one in law enforcement. There were just too many reasons why it couldn't—shouldn't—happen. The last thing she wanted to do was end up like her mother. It was much easier to just focus on her career and her independence. Her financial security. Knowing that she didn't have to rely on anyone—including a man—for anything. If she started to go down a different path, she couldn't guarantee those things. It was a risk she didn't think she could take.

"I realize you have every reason in the world not to trust me. But I want to earn your trust, Annie."

"This isn't about you, Caleb. I'm the one with issues. You shouldn't have to deal with my baggage. You don't deserve that. You have your own life to attend to."

He reached out and grabbed onto her hand. "But that's the thing, Annie. I find myself really enjoying the time we have together."

She sucked in a breath, trying to formulate her answer. But before she could respond, a loud pop burst through the silent evening. The next thing she knew, Caleb had pushed her down on the porch floor, covering her body with his own. She heard the dogs barking loudly from inside the house. Her heart pounded as fear tore through her. This was it. She could die right now. They both could die.

Another shot was fired and her entire body shook. Caleb lifted up off of her for one second and returned fire—getting off three shots in quick succession.

"Stay low!" He held onto her and pushed her toward the door. He reached up and grabbed the knob. "Go inside. Go to an interior room and lock yourself in. Do not come back out here. I'll come and get you once it's safe."

She listened to him as her pulse continued to race. The dogs were going crazy jumping and barking. They knew something was wrong. She did as he directed and moved toward the bathroom on the first floor. Buddy and Bailey followed her, sensing the imminent danger that surrounded them.

As she locked the three of them into the bathroom, she realized that fresh, hot tears were pouring down her face. Someone was trying to kill her. All because she'd witnessed a murder. She should've never been at the Perry's in the first place. Why had she needed to try that recipe so badly? This all could've been avoided. But now here she was, caught in the crossfire again.

She highly doubted that the bathroom door would keep her safe against an armed assailant, but she had no other option. Her mind flashbacked to the last time she had locked herself in a room trying to protect herself from danger. But this time was different, she reminded herself. This time she didn't have a gun, but she wasn't alone either. She had to count on Caleb to protect her. He was putting his life on the line for her. To defend her.

She huddled in the corner of the bathroom hugging tightly onto Buddy while Bailey stood guard by the door. She could feel the rapid beat of Buddy's heartbeat. But he was right there with her. Providing her comfort. As the minutes ticked by, she knew it hadn't been that long, but it felt like an eternity.

What if the gunman had killed Caleb? Taking a few deep breaths she had to calm down. *Lord, I can't get through this alone. I need You now to protect us from harm. Be with me, dear Lord.*

When she heard Caleb's voice calling to her from the other side of the door, relief flooded through her that he was alive. *Thank you, Lord.*

"Open the door, Annie. It's me."

Bailey and Buddy started barking when they heard Caleb's voice. Slowly, she stood up and tried to gather herself. She knew she looked like a hot mess.

She opened the door and gasped. Blood was streaked down Caleb's cheek. Instinctively, she reached out and touched his face. "You're bleeding."

"I got slashed by a tree branch in the backyard when I was chasing down the shooter. It's nothing serious."

It looked bad to her. "Are you sure?"

"Yes, I'm fine. I promise. I've had much worse than this."

"Did you get him?"

"No. He got away." He ran his hand through his hair. "I hate to do this to you, Annie, but we need to get out of here. It's not safe anymore."

"What about the dogs?"

"Mac's going to take them. I just called him on my way back inside, and he's on his way over here. Can you pack up your things?"

"Yes." She tried to process everything he was saying, but she was still in a state of shock. Seeing the blood that had run down his face made everything even more real.

"Annie," he said softly. "You know that I'd lay down my own life to protect you, right?"

His words broke her already fragile mental state and the tears started flowing freely. "Caleb, I don't know if I can handle all of this. Maybe I should just go away and hide on my own. All I'm doing is bringing danger to your doorstep."

"Absolutely, not."

"But what about your job? You can't just up and leave."

"My deputy is fully able to handle things here. He's had decades of experience as a police officer. You need me more right now."

And wasn't that the truth. If it weren't for Caleb, she wouldn't be alive. "I'll go start packing."

"Everything is going to be okay," Caleb said.

She could only pray that he was right.

* * *

Caleb gripped the wheel tightly as he drove through the night. He was worried about Annie. She'd barely spoken since they'd started driving. And he couldn't really blame her.

The situation at his house had been far too close. What had he been thinking, suggesting that they sit outside on the back porch? He'd allowed himself to let his guard down. He was a professional—not just in law enforcement, but also given his military background.

It occurred to him that his feelings for Annie were starting to cloud his judgment. He was usually so cautious and measured, but he had wanted to make her happy by going outside instead of focusing on her safety first. He wouldn't make that mistake again. One of the first lessons he'd learned in the military was that you couldn't make decisions based on emotions.

God, please give me guidance to get through this battle and to keep Annie safe from harm. I'm not strong enough to face another loss in my life right now.

"Do you know where we're going?" She finally broke the silence.

"Just taking it one step at a time. Wanted to put a little distance between us and Maxwell. I'll stop in a bit. I know you're exhausted."

"Me? What about you? I wasn't the one hunting down the shooter."

"My military training helps a lot with that. I can function on very little sleep. But we both need to be on the top of our games to deal with the threats coming at us."

"I've been doing a lot of thinking."

Uh oh, he thought. He wondered what she was about to say. "What's on your mind?"

"Why does Silva care so much about me? I'm just one woman. He has a huge criminal enterprise. What could he really fear from me?"

"Guys like Silva hold grudges and they don't like leaving loose ends. He wasn't there that night. So he doesn't know how much you heard and what you're going to do with the information. He has to be cautious. You could be a witness in a criminal trial that would implicate him. And he doesn't want to take that kind of chance. He has too much riding on it. There is big money in criminal enterprises like this, Annie. We're talking about millions of dollars."

"But I can't run my entire life," she said flatly.

"I'm not asking you to, but in the short term what happened tonight shows that you are a primary target of the Silva crime syndicate. They're not going to just let this go anytime soon. So we have to take action accordingly."

His phone rang and he saw that it was Mike calling. "I have to take this. It's my deputy."

He answered knowing that Mike would want to talk to him. Mac was supposed to have called Mike to fill him in on the situation.

"Caleb, hey, it's Mike."

"Did you talk to Mac?"

"Yes, and he told me about what happened. But we've got another problem. A big one."

"What happened?"

"The prisoners escaped."

"What? How?" Just when Caleb thought things couldn't really get much worse.

"McCoy tricked our officer on duty to open the cell door. McCoy was able to disarm the officer and knock him out. Then McCoy took the officer's keys and took Phil with him according to our video cam footage."

"This is not good," Caleb said. But at least they were on the road. McCoy wouldn't know where to find them. And then it occurred to him, what if McCoy was the shooter tonight? "Mike, what's the time stamp on the prison break video?"

"About eight o'clock tonight. I'm just calling you now because I only found out about it a bit ago and was trying to get everything under control and make sure the facility was secured. Our officer was knocked out cold for a long time. And then Mac called and told me that you were on the run. What's going on here, Caleb?"

"I can't go into all the details. It's not safe for Annie to be in Maxwell right now. But I need you to hold down the fort while I'm gone."

"Are you sure you need to be doing this alone? This all sounds very dangerous. I don't think we've ever had a jailbreak in Maxwell."

"Don't worry about me. Just keep your focus on the town. I need to know that everything will be taken care of and our citizens will be safe."

Mike sighed. "I've only been an officer here for decades, Caleb."

"I know. And that's why I'm entrusting this to you."

"I've got it under control. But what should we do about the escaped prisoners?"

"Call Mac and get him involved. I think they'll be long gone. Especially when they realize that Annie is no longer in town."

"All right. I'll give Mac a ring and make sure all our officers are on the lookout. Be careful out there. These guys seem like the type to shoot first and ask questions later."

"Thanks, Mike. I'm so thankful that I can count on you." He ended the call and took a deep breath.

"What was that all about?" Annie asked.

"McCoy escaped and took Phil with him."

"Oh no. He might kill Phil."

"Yeah, once he got clear of the surveillance video, he might have taken Phil out right then and there. And there's a possibility, given the timing of the escape that McCoy was the shooter at my house."

"I can't believe all of this."

"Just hang tight. We'll figure out a plan." He looked in his rearview mirror and noticed the headlights that had been behind them were getting closer and closer. He realized that he might be paranoid at this point, but a sinking feeling in his gut had him accelerating to see how the car behind would respond.

"Why are you speeding up all of a sudden?" Annie asked.

"Make sure your seatbelt is secure."

"Caleb, what's going on? You're scaring me."

"We may have a tail." It was just as he feared. The SUV behind them was gaining ground, matching his speed with each acceleration. He pushed down the gas pedal.

Annie turned around. "Caleb, they're going to hit us!"

He pushed the gas all the way down, but he didn't have to look in his mirror to know that the impact was going to come any second.

Annie screamed as they were rammed from behind by the large SUV.

He feared that if he didn't make a sudden move the next hit was going to get them both hurt. And he had to do his best to try to shield Annie from this killer. "Brace yourself!" He gripped the wheel harder and did the only thing he could, taking a hard right and ran off the road.

CHAPTER SIX

Caleb knew he was taking a risk when he made the move to suddenly turn off the road into the wooded area. He pressed the gas and made it about three quarters of a mile before things went from bad to worse. By the time he saw the large tree in front of him, it was too late. The impact was hard enough to deploy the airbags.

He withstood the hit, but his first thoughts went to Annie.

"Annie," he said. He unbuckled his seatbelt and looked over at her. Fear like nothing he'd ever felt ripped through him. "Annie," he said again louder. But still no response from her.

He reached over and checked for a pulse in her neck. It was fast and strong. She must have been knocked out by the impact, but at least she was alive. He hated to move her, but he couldn't take the risk that they were followed by the SUV into the woods.

Without wasting another second, he went around to the other side of the car and pulled her gently out—cradling her in his arms. He was thankful that he'd continued his military style workout routine so he would be able to carry her without any issue if they needed to hike a distance.

He needed to get Annie to safety. Then he'd come back and gather up the rest of their stuff. Just as he started walking with Annie in his arms, he saw the headlights approaching. He ran a few steps and placed Annie down on the ground behind some tall trees to provide her cover. Then he crouched down beside her, ready to act.

The area they were in right now was wooded so that the assailant would be forced to get out of his car if he was going to try to get to them. He couldn't drive straight up to where they were. And when he got out of his car, Caleb would be ready to pounce. He pulled his gun out and waited as he heard the SUV stop. The headlights illuminating the area.

If the man in the SUV was McCoy, he knew from previous experience that McCoy would be willing and able to use lethal force. The only lights were those coming from the SUV. But the darkness actually worked in his favor. He'd done so many missions in the dead of night—although in the military he would have had his night vision aids. Now he'd just have to improvise. His opponent was going to be in the same boat. The fact that the attacker was following them into the woods let him know his intentions were deadly. There was no doubt that McCoy had received the kill order from Silva. And McCoy probably worried that if he failed, then it would be his hide on the line.

He could see enough of the man getting out of the SUV to recognize by the silhouette that it was McCoy. Caleb planned to make sure that McCoy wasn't able to go through with his mission. But regardless, Caleb was still a police officer—an officer of the law, not a mercenary like McCoy. He couldn't just shoot him without it being in self-defense or in defense of Annie. He had to try to attempt to take him in. Unlike the officers that had betrayed Annie years ago, Caleb had vowed to serve and protect with honor.

But if McCoy pulled his gun, Caleb would have no hesitation in acting. McCoy started walking toward the abandoned vehicle. Caleb's best opportunity would be to jump him from behind.

McCoy left his SUV running so the headlights worked in Caleb's favor. Making sure that Annie was still safely hidden behind the large tree, he then started to inch forward. Timing his steps with McCoy. This wasn't the first time that Caleb had engaged in a sneak attack. But as he took a step forward a flashback hit him hard. Vivid pictures ran through his head.

He was back in the mountains of Afghanistan. Dirt filled his mouth. His arm ached as the bullet grazed through his flesh and fresh blood poured out of him. He could hear the whirling noise of the chopper pounding in his ears. The sound of AK-47 fire ripping through the night. The final scream from his brother in arms before the life left his body—Caleb helpless to do anything but evacuate with the rest of his SEAL team that had just arrived at the scene.

A loud crunching sound brought Caleb back to reality—but not quickly enough.

McCoy grabbed onto Caleb's arm catching him off guard, his gun dropping from his right hand to the ground. The physical contact jarred Caleb back to life though and he fought back. With a swift upper cut that connected to McCoy's jaw, followed by a kick squarely in the solar plexus, knocking McCoy back a few steps.

Caleb used the moment to grab his gun from the ground. "Hands up, McCoy. I will shoot."

McCoy moved slowly. But Caleb knew that the man had a gun, probably in his waistband. If McCoy went for it, Caleb would have no choice but to shoot.

"This isn't about you, man," McCoy said. "Just hand over the girl and walk away. She isn't worth the trouble."

"You're wrong about that. Keep your hands up."

"One thing you've let me know over the short time I've known you is that you're the type to do the right thing." McCoy turned around and took off running into the woods. McCoy knew that there was no way Caleb would shoot him while he was retreating. And he was right. Caleb wouldn't shoot a man in the back that was fleeing the scene.

Caleb started in pursuit, but McCoy was fast. And even more than that, Caleb couldn't afford to leave Annie alone. He chased him for about a quarter mile, but then quickly turned back.

He couldn't believe he'd had a flashback. He hadn't had one in almost a year. And it almost cost him his life and Annie's too. And that would've been another unforgivable mistake.

***

Annie tasted blood in her mouth and opened her eyes, blinking a few times. She looked around in the darkness and was disoriented. Where in the world was she? Nothing seemed familiar. She took in a breath and it seemed like she was outside.

Her pulse quickened as she tried to figure out what was going on. Then she remembered that they had been hit from behind by the SUV and that Caleb had made a sudden turn off the road. But then what happened? She couldn't remember a thing.

She wasn't in the car anymore. Looking around she realized that she had been propped up against a large tree in the woods. And where was Caleb? What if he was hurt? Or worse? *Dear Lord, help me.*

She tried to move and her body ached. Especially her head. She reached up to her temple as it pounded. Being out in the middle of the woods didn't seem like somewhere she needed to be.

"Caleb, are you there?"

No answer. She didn't know if she should stay put or try to get away. It occurred to her that Caleb had to have gotten her out of the car. Because if it had been one of Silva's men, then they would've killed her. They wouldn't have left her behind a tree in the middle of the woods. She wouldn't still be breathing right now if Silva's men had gotten to her. But that didn't mean that Caleb was all right. What if he was injured and needed her?

"Caleb," she said, raising her voice louder this time. Panic started to set in as there was still no answer. Where could he be? Should she try to find him? It was dark, but there was a bit of light coming from the opposite direction, from a car that was a couple of hundred feet away.

She tried again. "Caleb!"

"Annie, I'll be right there," he said.

A huge flood of relief came over her as she tried to stand, but stumbled, as her legs gave out on her. She grabbed onto the tree to try to steady herself and fight off the sick feeling in her stomach. With only the limited light, she couldn't see him. After a moment, she sensed his presence in front of her as he reached out and touched her cheek.

"I'm here, Annie. How're you feeling?"

"I'm okay. What in the world happened?" She realized she needed to slow down her breathing, as she was about to hyperventilate. She couldn't help but grab onto his arm to steady herself.

"Are you lightheaded?"

"Maybe a little." Or a lot. The longer she stood the more uneasy she got. She didn't want to show him all of her weakness, though. She would just have to tough this out like she had everything else.

"I think you hit your head when I ran into the tree. I'm sorry, I didn't see it until it was too late. The airbags came out, but the impact knocked you out. I need to get you to a hospital and get checked out."

"No. I'll be fine. What happened to the person in the SUV?"

"It was McCoy. He followed us out here. He and I got into a fight but he got away. I wasn't going to shoot him while he was on the run. I pursued, but I didn't want to leave you alone, so I circled back to get you."

"So you're sure he's gone?"

"Yes, but we're going to use his SUV to get out of here. My car isn't in any condition to drive out of here since I smashed it into the tree."

"What do we do now?" Her mind felt like mush as she asked questions.

"We get another car ASAP, because we don't know if McCoy's SUV has a tracking device on it. I'll call Mac from the road and get his help. But we can't stay here in the woods. I want to get back on the road right now."

"This is never going to end, is it?" She heard her voice crack as she asked. "Caleb, I'm afraid that I can't handle all of this." She was near the breaking point—both physically and emotionally. Her head pounded from the accident and that wasn't helping.

He wrapped his arms around her and brought her into a gentle embrace. "I've got you, Annie. Lean on me."

She fell into him and relied on his strength to hold her up. Caleb had kept her safe so far. But deep in her heart she was still afraid because she didn't know if anyone could truly keep her safe.

***

Annie had tossed and turned, barely sleeping. When she did fall asleep, she had nightmares—a mix of the shooting from her past and the car accident. Which really wasn't an accident at all. And it had left her with a major headache plus some other pain and soreness in her neck. But she'd refused to go to the hospital because it was all just too much. And she knew there was no way she was going to take any pain medication. Given her mother's history of drug abuse, she refused to take any painkillers for fear of ending up like her mom. She'd rather face the pain than take that risk.

She and Caleb were at an extended stay hotel with adjoining rooms in the middle of a South Georgia town. They had driven south from Atlanta and ended up there to try to get some much needed rest and to regroup.

Caleb had even seemed a bit off after what had happened in the woods. She couldn't expect him to be invincible. He wasn't superman—he was just a man. He had his own weaknesses and emotional reactions just like she did. It was just that he was much better equipped than she was to maneuver through this dangerous maze. So when she could see that he had wavered a little last night, that's when she knew they were in big trouble.

When a loud knock sounded on her hotel room door, she jumped and immediately went on guard. Slowly she walked to the door taking careful steps with the soreness. She looked through the peephole. A woman with long blond hair and a dark haired man were on the other side. They must have the wrong room.

"Caleb, are you in there?" the tall man asked.

If the couple was asking for Caleb, then they couldn't be sent by Silva, could they?

"Who are you?" she asked without opening the door.

"I'm FBI agent Gabe Marino and this is my wife Hope. Caleb's brother called me to help. Can you please let us in?"

Just then the adjoining door opened and Caleb walked through it. He'd obviously been in a deep sleep—his hair was tousled and there were dark circles under his eyes, only fueling her speculation that last night had bothered him almost as much as it had bothered her.

"You can open it." Caleb walked toward her, and she opened the door as he directed.

Gabe and Hope walked in. Gabe wore a deep frown, but Hope looked her directly in the eyes and gave a warm smile.

Hope then walked over to her and offered her hand. "I'm Hope. I hear that you've had quite a week."

"Yeah. It's been rough."

"Did Mac call you?" Caleb asked.

"Yes," Gabe responded. "Late last night as we were driving back up to Maxwell from Florida. You were on our way, so we wanted to stop by. I need to hear about everything that's happened."

Annie's head was still pounding, and she started rubbing her temples again. She needed coffee, like right now, or she wouldn't make it. She walked to the kitchenette area and started making some coffee.

Hope followed right behind her. "Why don't you two guys go into Caleb's room and catch up while Annie and I get to know each other," Hope said.

Once again, Hope gave her a sweet smile. It was like she somehow understood that Annie was near a breaking point.

"Sure," Gabe said. "We'll be right next door if you need us." The two men went into Caleb's room leaving her alone with Hope.

She let out a breath. "Thank you. I don't think I could handle another recitation of all the awful things that have happened to me."

"I know you may find this hard to believe." Hope's brown eyes were filled with kindness. "But I can relate to what you're going through because I had a very scary series of events happen to me when I came down to Maxwell a little over a year ago for a trial."

"Really?" She was a bit skeptical that anyone could really understand what the past few days had been like, but she was willing to listen.

"Yes. I'm a lawyer. Now I work at a small law firm in Maxwell, but at the time, I was working for a big firm in New York."

"Please, have a seat while we wait on the coffee and tell me what happened," Annie said.

She took a seat and waited for Hope to explain.

"It's a long story. Basically, I was working on a case where the client was involved in some illegal activities. When I realized what was happening, I became a target. People I thought I could trust ended up trying to kill me. It shook me down to the core." Hope paused. "I was physically attacked multiple times. If it hadn't have been for Gabe, I wouldn't be alive sitting here with you today. And Caleb also played a critical role in keeping me safe. I owe so much to him. So when we heard that the two of you were in trouble, there was no way we were just going to go home. Caleb was there when we needed him, and now we want to be there for him. And for you."

"I'm so sorry that you went through all of that." Annie's heart hurt for the woman sitting across the kitchen table from her.

"It all worked out in the end. Including me falling in love with a wonderful man. But I had some real low points. And I imagine you might be having one of those valleys right now."

Hope's openness and honesty put Annie at ease. "Thank you so much for sharing. You're completely right. I feel like I'm really at the breaking point. After last night when we were run off the road, I hit my head and haven't felt sturdy since then. And that doesn't begin to explain all that has happened."

Hope reached out and took her hand. "I know it may not seem like it right now, but there is an end to all of this. God is still there beside you. He hasn't abandoned you. And He won't. You're still here, aren't you?"

"I keep telling myself that but sometimes it's hard to see that amidst all the danger. This experience has really tested my faith."

"You'll persevere. I know it. You're not alone and I'm sure Gabe and Caleb can come up with a plan. They work really well together. And of course, I'm not in law enforcement, but I can pitch in anyway that makes sense. Even if it's just to be a shoulder to lean on."

"I'm glad you're here. Although I'm sure this isn't how you envisioned coming back to town after your honeymoon."

"We roll with the punches. Given Gabe's job as an FBI agent, I know there are risks involved and I have to be ready for anything."

Annie hadn't spent much time with women developing friendships, but this conversation with Hope was one of the most normal things that had happened to her in a while. "And what about you? How do you like being a lawyer?"

Hope leaned in toward her. "I absolutely love it. I can't imagine myself doing anything else. And once I was able to work at the law firm in Maxwell, it really made my career complete. I get to do what I want to do, but I'm also not sacrificing my sanity working in New York City at a mega firm."

"That's a big change from New York to Maxwell."

"Yeah, and let me tell you, at first I was totally against the idea of changing my life. I thought I was a city girl through and through and that Maxwell didn't have anything for me. But boy, was I wrong. Sometimes exactly what you think you don't want is really what you need. And that was the case for me."

Annie couldn't help but ask her about Silva. "I guess you don't have any experience with the Silva crime organization?"

"No. I don't practice criminal law. But that type of thing is right up Gabe's alley at the FBI. That's specifically the kind of work he does. It's good that we're back now and can assist Caleb."

"Maybe he'll be able to help us then."

"Definitely. Gabe values his friendship with Caleb. There's no place he'd rather be right now."

"Thanks for saying that." Hope seemed so sincere. Like she actually cared about what Annie had to say and understood some of the struggles that she was going through. And as much as it surprised Annie, she was glad to be proven wrong about Hope being able to empathize with her.

"I hear that you're a chef. I can't cook a thing." Hope laughed.

"I'm sure I could teach you a few simple dishes. It's all about having fresh ingredients and then knowing how to season." It would be fun to actually cook with someone who wasn't an experienced chef.

Hope lifted up her hand. "You don't understand. I'm the world's worst cook."

"You have more important things to do—like being a lawyer."

"No. What you do is important, too. And it takes a lot of skill. I've always admired people who had cooking abilities. I just happen to have none."

"Well, I'd love to cook with you sometime. Just give it a shot."

"That's a deal."

"I would think that being an attorney is very exciting."

Hope grinned. "It's not as glamorous as it looks on TV. There's a lot of grunt work. But I enjoy going to trial. That's my favorite part, though it doesn't happen as much as I would like."

Annie poured them each a cup of coffee and realized that her head was no longer hurting as bad as it had been.

***

"Talk to me, Caleb." Gabe's dark eyes were focused on him.

"What else do you want to know?" He felt like Gabe was about to conduct an interrogation. And he couldn't blame him. He knew the entire situation seemed sketchy.

"I know we've been through the facts, but I need to know what's going on in your head, and how you're dealing with all of this, because I've got some serious concerns about you going on the run with Annie. I don't think you're fully aware what you're up against. And one man versus the Silva network doesn't sound like very good odds to me."

"This wasn't my plan by choice. More like a necessity. After the shooting at my house, I knew I had to get Annie out of there. I had no idea that we would be followed. I'm trying to juggle multiple balls in the air right now, but my primary focus has to be on keeping Annie safe. Which means I can't really investigate what is going on with Silva and why he seems to have this unhealthy obsession with Annie."

Gabe nodded. "There has to be a missing piece here. Yeah, Silva wants to get rid of Annie because she was a witness to a hit that he ordered, and heard an incriminating conversation, but there has to be something deeper. Guys like Silva don't put this much effort into something like this. We've got to dig deeper and figure out what else is going on."

"Given the most recent events, I tend to agree with you. Normally we'd have the FBI working that angle. Put her in protective custody. But with the intel that we have that someone in the FBI is on Silva's payroll, I just couldn't take that chance. Not with Annie's life."

"I don't want to overstep here, but you and I have been friends for many years."

"Uh oh. What is it?" Caleb asked, although he had a good idea where this conversation was going.

"Is there something going on between you and Annie?" Caleb paused. "But before you answer, I'm the last one to cast judgment on you, given what happened between me and Hope. I just want to make sure that you're thinking clearly. That's all. I remember all too well what it was like to make decisions in the heat of the moment based on my heart and not my head."

He was close enough with Caleb that he could be honest. "There isn't anything between us. But I'd be lying if I said I wasn't interested. I realize, though, that this isn't the best time to try to start a relationship. And beyond that, there are some issues that we'd have to deal with. Things I really don't feel like it's my place to go into. Not to mention my own hang-ups."

Gabe took a step forward. "I would never ask you to divulge things that Annie told you in confidence. But this is a highly dangerous situation and everyone needs to be fully engaged. Silva's organization is powerful, and as a man, Tim Silva is ruthless. And his business partners are equally as threatening. It wouldn't be safe to go further south into Florida because his cousin covers Florida, and he's just as bad. If Silva is taking this drastic of action, he has spread the word to all of his network partners."

"So what do you suggest?"

"Hunkering down in a safe house would be my best suggestion."

"Except we don't have a safe house that's actually safe."

"We can find one. I have a friend at the DEA. They would have an interest in this situation, given Silva's drug operations. I'll put in a call and see what I can do."

Caleb let out a breath. This was the best news he'd had in a while. "Thanks, man. I don't know how to thank you. My back was really up against the wall."

"You had my back when I needed it. I'm happy to return the favor."

***

Annie watched as Caleb and Gabe walked back into her room. The men joined them in the kitchen. Caleb actually seemed much more relaxed than before. Maybe the talk with Gabe had been productive.

"I made coffee, if you guys would like any," she said.

"That would be great." Caleb took her up on her offer and poured himself and Gabe a cup.

"So, anything we need to know about?" Annie asked. She was anxious to hear about what the men had discussed, especially if they had developed a way out of this entire mess.

"Gabe actually has a contact at the Drug Enforcement Agency. He's going to talk to him about trying to secure a safe house for us."

"Really?" Annie asked. This was great news and totally unexpected. A safe house was exactly what they needed.

"Yeah. We talked about it, and I think it's better to hide out than to try to outrun these guys," Caleb said.

"I'll call my DEA contact right away. Hope, why don't you come with me while I go make these calls in Caleb's room."

"If you need anything, just let me know." Hope squeezed her hand, and the kind act brought her a moment of comfort. She hoped that she would get to spend more time with this woman. The idea of having a friend appealed to her more right now than it ever had.

Hope and Gabe went into Caleb's room, leaving her alone with Caleb. Unexpectedly, he pulled her up out of her seat and wrapped his arms around her.

"I promise you that we'll figure this out," he said, his voice calm and soothing.

As he held her tightly in his arms, she realized just how much she had come to depend on him. An unlikely ally in this fight. A fight that didn't seem to have an end as each moment brought another challenge and another deadly threat.

"Caleb, I'm sorry that I'm not stronger about all of this."

"There's no need for you to apologize, Annie, because what you fail to see is that you are beyond strong. You've kept it together from day one. From the moment you had the presence of mind to get out of Doc Perry's house and avoid being taken by McCoy, you've been fighting back each step of the way. You've shown that no matter what the challenge, you'll rise to the occasion."

"I don't see myself like that." She couldn't believe that he saw her that way, because inside, she felt full of fear.

"Well, that's the way I see you."

She continued to hold onto Caleb, though she knew a million different reasons that she shouldn't lean on him so much. But at that moment, none of that mattered. The only thing that mattered was that he was there by her side when she needed him the most. That he continued to put his life on the line for her—a woman he'd only known a short time.

As she looked up into his big blue eyes, she gained strength from him. When he leaned down and gently pressed his lips to hers, she felt shaky again—but this time in a good way. Like she was floating on a cloud. The spark was undeniable, unlike anything she'd ever experienced.

Was this what it was like to really have feelings for someone?

When he pulled back from the kiss, the stubble on his chin tickled her cheek. She didn't want this moment to end.

Caleb took a step back from her just as Gabe and Hope walked back into the room.

"We're a go on the safe house," he said. "Let's get you out of here."

CHAPTER SEVEN

Caleb hadn't been thinking when he had kissed Annie. It just happened. And he had been worried about her reaction. But when he had opened his eyes and locked onto hers, there was no mistaking that she had felt something there, too. Something that neither of them seemed to think was a good idea, but that hadn't stopped him from acting.

The larger issue was whether he should even allow himself to develop these feelings for Annie. He knew he was a guarded guy when it came to his emotions. But being in this situation with Annie had totally messed up his equilibrium. The emotions he was so used to having completely in check weren't any more. It was like she had the only key to the box where he'd stored up all of his feelings.

He'd already made one dangerous mistake because of what he felt for her. He couldn't afford for that to happen again. But even telling himself all of that, he hadn't been able to stop from kissing her. Because right then and there, it felt like the right thing to do.

They backtracked and drove a few hours north, headed toward Atlanta, and arrived at the address provided to Gabe by the DEA contact who they were supposed to be meeting at the safe house in the Atlanta suburbs.

Once Gabe had given the all clear to enter the safe house, Caleb escorted Annie inside.

A tall man with dark hair and a leather jacket met them inside. This had to be the DEA agent.

"I'm agent Kane Sloan with the DEA." Kane outstretched his hand and made introductions with everyone.

"Are you sure this location is secure?" Caleb asked. It was his job to question Kane because he couldn't take anymore unnecessary risks. The fact that Gabe trusted Kane was the only reason they were here. But Caleb still had to confirm and hear it from Kane's own lips.

"Yes. I personally reserved this safe house for another project I'm working on. I just won't use it while you're here."

"We appreciate you jumping in to help," Caleb said.

Kane nodded. "I would like to be able to talk to Annie about what she witnessed at the Perry house. Gabe briefed me, but I'd like to hear it from her." Then Kane turned his attention to Annie.

Immediately Caleb's protective instincts kicked in. The last thing Annie needed to deal with right now was an interrogation. "Annie's had a rough day. Maybe she can fill you in later. I'm sure she wants to get settled in."

"No," Annie said. "That's okay, Caleb. I appreciate everything Kane is doing for me." She looked over at Kane. "I will try to help out in any way that I can."

Kane smiled at Annie and Caleb couldn't help but feel a tinge of jealousy. He'd only met Kane two minutes ago, and he was already wondering if Kane would be a better match for Annie than him. He had to keep himself in check.

He listened as Annie told Kane all she knew about what happened that night at Doc Perry's house and what she'd heard about Tim Silva. Which admittedly wasn't a whole lot. Doc had gotten in over his head with a very dangerous man.

"Well, just like everyone else, the DEA has their own angle when it comes to the Silva organization. Right now, the DEA is focused on trying to tie Silva to some large drug ops that have occurred down in south Florida over the past few months," Kane said. "Silva's organization has reached a new level. They're trying to tangle with some of the established groups that have been around much longer. Which is why you'll be safe here until we can figure out the best course of action."

Caleb had to bite his tongue. He didn't like Kane stepping in and taking charge. But he also knew that he needed the DEA's support especially given the FBI situation. He should just be quiet and thankful that they now had a safe house. "Do you have any intel on the FBI agent working with the organization?"

"No. But we've kept our DEA operation walled off from FBI for a variety of reasons," Kane said.

"Turf war," Gabe said. "Don't try to act like it isn't."

"But in this instance, Gabe, it works in your favor," Kane said. "I'm not the enemy here."

"Same here," Gabe said. "This is going to take a team effort."

"Thanks, everyone," Caleb replied. "It will require us all pitching in. And, Kane, this safe house is a huge contribution." He looked over at a weary Annie. "But I do think we would probably like to try to get some rest. It's been a long couple of days for us."

Annie looked over at him and gave him a small smile—but it was big enough to remind him of the kiss they'd shared earlier.

"I'm going to take Hope back home to Maxwell. But if you want me to come back after that, I will."

"I don't think that's necessary," Caleb said. "We're off the grid right now. We just need to make sure it stays that way."

"I'll check on you two in the morning," Kane said. "Here is a burner phone I picked up for you."

Caleb had already taken out his SIM card from his phone earlier. He was glad to have a burner now. "Thanks for everything," he said.

"No problem. Lock up and watch your back," Kane said.

***

Annie watched as everyone else left the safe house, leaving her alone with Caleb. A wave of exhaustion washed over her. They'd basically been on the run for the past twenty-four hours and it was difficult for her.

He walked over to her after he locked the front door and set the alarm system per Kane's earlier instruction. He gently took her hand in his. "I know this is completely crazy, Annie. But at least now we have some support from the DEA. And having this safe house is clutch."

"Do you think it's really safe?"

"I'm not going to lie to you. Nothing is a hundred percent right now. But this is as close as we're going to get. The only people that know we're here are people we know we can trust. It's why we're keeping the circle so small."

She hadn't had much time to fully process the kiss between them. But as he stood there now holding her hand, it felt so natural. "Speaking of that. Don't you need to check in again with Mac and Gabby?"

"I will. I just wanted to make sure you had everything you needed first. Talk about a whirlwind."

She nodded her head. "I think some sleep will make a big difference. Maybe I'll finally get some, now that we have at least a little more stability than before."

He dropped her hand and brushed a lock of hair out of her eyes. At his touch, she wondered if this could even be real.

"Pick whatever room you want and I'll choose one close by. I don't want to stay on different floors. Just in case."

"Sure." She didn't like the sound of those contingencies. But she appreciated that he was on high alert. The events of the past days let her know that danger was lurking around every corner.

"And are we okay?" he asked.

"What do you mean?"

"I don't know if I overstepped with you. We really haven't had a chance to talk about it."

Yeah, that kiss was everything. She tried to find the words to respond. "I'm okay if you're okay," she replied.

He smiled and her heart warmed. "I'm more than okay on that front. It's everything else that we need to get squared away."

Although a bit of doubt and fear started to creep into her mind. Should she really think that something between them was possible? She'd been cautious of relationships for over a decade. And now she was considering what? What did he want out of all of this? Was she even capable of having a normal romantic relationship?

"I can see the wheels turning in your mind," he said. "Talk to me, Annie."

She wondered how much she should share with him. He already knew she had scars from her past, so she might as well be honest about her lack of experience in the romance department. "I'm not really good at this whole thing, whatever it is that is happening between you and me. I don't date."

"Like ever?"

"Nothing of any substance. It's just been easier that way. It's not like I had a good role model in that area. So I have been much more hesitant than most people. The last thing I want to do is repeat the cycles of my past."

He took a step closer to her. "You're not your mother, Annie."

"My mind tells me that, but it's harder to convince the heart that I am really capable of living differently than she did. You know?"

"Why don't you let me help you then? I've also put up barriers around myself for years. We can work through this together, can't we? If you just give me a chance, then maybe we'll tear down barriers together."

Her pulse quickened—a combination of fear and longing for something more. But there was a voice in her head telling her that she was foolish to think she'd have a normal relationship. "Can we talk about this later? I'm exhausted." Her shoulders slumped a little.

"Of course. I know you're tired. Go get settled in. I'll check on you in a little bit."

"All right." She felt a tinge of disappointment that he didn't push the issue further. But he was doing exactly what she had asked. She couldn't blame him for respecting her wishes. She started to walk away, eager for a moment of respite, but Caleb's burner phone rang. She stopped as he answered the call.

"Gabby, I'm putting you on speaker. I'm here with Annie."

"Hey, you two. I got the burner number from Gabe. He just filled me in on what's been going on. I can't believe all of this. You sure that you're both okay?"

"Yes, we're fine," he said. "Annie got busted up a bit when we hit the tree trying to evade the SUV that was stalking us, but she's been bouncing back really well."

It was nice to hear him say that, because she didn't feel like she was handling anything well at all.

"Thank the Lord that it wasn't any worse, then. From what I understand, the two of you could very well be dead right now."

Gabby's words sent another shot of fear through her.

"But we're not," Caleb said. "We're both safe."

"I've been busy investigating the Silva network," Gabby said. "Unfortunately, Phil Perry was right. There is a move to expand the drug operations out of Atlanta and into certain suburbs and small towns, especially on the storage side. I also think I found a warehouse in Maxwell that Silva's people have purchased under the name of one of his many shell companies. So I'm going to keep an eye on the activity there. I know you were concerned about the organization's presence in Maxwell. Hopefully I can get some evidence that will lead you to conduct a police investigation and shut him down before he gets too far off the ground. I'll want to make sure that they are fully operational in the warehouse before I make any sudden moves, because I don't want to spook them."

"Gabby, you should step back," he said.

"Why in the world would I do that? I'm finally getting somewhere," she said.

Annie could hear the frustration in Gabby's elevated voice.

"This is way too dangerous now, Gabriella."

"Don't you even go there, Caleb. You know that only mom and dad used to call me that name."

"And since mom and dad are no longer with us, I have to be the parent here and step in."

"It's unfair for you to do that," Gabby responded.

"This isn't one of your usual PI jobs. If Silva finds out you're snooping around, he won't give a second thought about having one of his guys, like McCoy, take you out. I can't be worrying about you getting in the crosshairs while Annie is also being targeted. It's just too much. Again, I'm asking you to back off of this. Now."

Annie started to put the pieces together. Caleb hadn't mentioned anything about his parents before. And now she understood why. They were dead. Just like her mom. She'd been so focused on her own family drama, that she hadn't even bothered to ask him about his parents. She should've never been so focused only on herself.

"You wouldn't be saying this to me if it was Mac doing it," Gabby shot back. "In fact, you'd be asking for his help. Encouraging him to find out more information. Do you realize how that hurts me? I'm a big girl. I can do the job I was trained to do."

"Actually, under these set of circumstances, I'd be worried about him too. But at the end of the day, Gabby, you're my baby sister. And it's my job to protect you at all costs. Even when it ticks you off that I'm trying to do so."

"Are you sure you aren't the one who hit your head in the accident? I'm a PI. I do a lot of dangerous assignments all the time. And you've never told me not to do my job before. Ever."

"And that should tell you a lot right there. This is on another level. I'm asking you to do this for me. Please let this go. At least for now."

Gabby let out a loud sigh. "Only because I can tell that you'll be worried nonstop if I don't, and we can't afford to have you distracted right now. I'll fill Mac in on everything I know and go from there."

"Thanks, Gabby."

Gabby hung up without saying anything else.

Caleb looked directly at her. "Gabby's great at her job. I don't doubt her abilities at all. But I can't help but worry about something happening to her. And I just couldn't handle that," Caleb said. "I couldn't handle losing her."

As she watched him, she saw some level of vulnerability. "I didn't know about your parents. Look at me." She threw her hands up. "I've been so self absorbed. It's completely embarrassing."

"You don't need to apologize. You've had every right to be focused on yourself given all that has happened. And it isn't like I'm the type of person to put it all out there."

"Even though I guess I haven't acted like it, I do really want to hear about you and your family, Caleb. What happened to your mom and dad?"

"Dad died of a heart attack right after I graduated high school. Mom was never the same after that. She had a stroke and passed away five years after he did."

"I'm so sorry."

"It's probably one of the reasons I'm so tight with Gabby and Mac. We had to get through all of that together. The three of us are super close, but we will butt heads because we are all very stubborn and independent. But I'm not going to take chances in a situation like this. Gabby might be mad at me now, but she won't stay that way forever. I'd rather have her mad than dead."

A chill shot down her back. "Will she actually listen to you?"

"I'd usually say no, but since she said she would this time, I think she will. No doubt she's on the phone with Mac right now trying to convince him to help her. Or at the very least complaining to him about how unreasonable I'm being."

"She just wants to be useful. I get that. I wish I could do more. Sometimes I feel like I'm just getting in the way and creating more problems for you."

"You're doing great, Annie." He paused. "And I know you're exhausted. We got sidetracked because of Gabby's call. You should go pick yourself a room and try to get settled in."

"Sounds good." Yes, she could use a few minutes alone and the much needed rest.

***

Once Annie left the room, Caleb let out a breath. With everything that was going on, and now with Gabby putting herself in the line of fire, he could feel his anxiety level rising. He internalized most of his emotions, but as the threats ramped up it was becoming more difficult to appear totally cool on the outside. But he didn't want to cause Annie any more concern than was needed. She knew they were in a life-threatening situation. He didn't need to compound that.

But the discussion with Gabby had led to a talk with Annie that he was glad he was able to have, because it allowed her to see another piece of him. He had just opened up about one of the most painful experiences of his life—the death of his parents—which would be rough for anyone who had lost their parents.

If only it was just that, though. Because he hadn't completely expressed why he was so worried about Gabby's well-being. He'd taken the first step, but there was a lot more. Losing his teammate in Afghanistan had forever changed him. The guilt still ate at him. If he was being honest with himself, he didn't think he'd make it if he lost someone else so soon that he loved.

So yes, he might be overprotective of Gabby, and he might have been a little controlling in his response, but it was only because deep down he was afraid of experiencing another loss. Afraid of his ability to cope with grief again right now.

It would've probably been the perfect opportunity to lay it all out there. Not just the death of his parents, but also what happened in Afghanistan. But the thought of trying to verbalize what happened to another person didn't seem possible. At least not yet. Although the fact that he was even thinking about it made him consider that maybe it was time to face the truth. To talk about the unspeakable. He wanted to be able to let Annie see his entire self—all the bruises and scars of his past. Maybe then she'd understand that he was just as broken as she was.

He made sure the downstairs was secure and that he knew the ins and outs of the safe house. He gave his deputy Mike Ramsey a call because he needed to keep him updated. And he also needed Mike's help.

When Mike answered, Caleb was relieved to be able to catch him up. "It's best for me not to give all the details, but a DEA contact came through for us and I'm in a safe place with Annie. I need you to do something for me, though."

"Sure, whatever you need," Mike said.

"I need you to keep an eye on Gabby. I think that she believes she's going to be able to help me with this case, but I worry she's going to get into trouble with Silva. I can't afford to have something happen to her."

"Say no more. I'll keep an eye out, but make sure that I'm discreet, because I know she'll freak out at both of us if she thinks I'm babysitting."

"Thanks, man. I'll keep you posted." His phoned beeped. "Look, I need to run. Mac is calling. And you can reach me on this number if you need me. It's a burner."

"You got it."

He switched over to answer Mac's call.

"Caleb," Mac said.

"Yeah."

"I've got some bad news."

"What now?"

"Phil Perry's body was just found. He was murdered."

CHAPTER EIGHT

aleb knew that Silva was determined to get rid of anyone and everyone who could tie him to Doc Perry's murder. He sat in the living room of the safe house with Gabe and Annie. He was about to break the news to Annie and feared how she was going to handle it. She'd already been through so much. But he'd told her that he wasn't going to keep her in the dark, and it was better for her to know all the facts.

"Okay," she said. "By the frowns on both of your faces, I'm assuming you have some bad news for me. So you might as well just rip the Band-Aid off."

"You want to tell her?" Gabe asked.

Caleb nodded. Yes, this was his responsibility. He wasn't going to push it off on his friend. "I'm sorry to have to tell you this, but Phil Perry's body was discovered."

She sucked in a breath. "He was killed?"

"Yes. The medical examiner hasn't given official cause of death yet, but it was clearly a homicide."

"McCoy killed him," she said in a matter of fact way.

"That's the most likely scenario," Caleb said. "And there's a manhunt for McCoy right now led by the Atlanta PD and assisted by the FBI. It's not ideal given the fact that we believe someone on the inside is on Silva's payroll."

Gabe leaned forward in his chair. "The possibility of a rogue FBI agent obviously presents a problem especially as it relates to

Annie's security. But one agent probably can't sabotage a wide-spread manhunt. There are too many different people involved, and he wouldn't want to blow his cover. Especially since Silva has probably already decided that McCoy is expendable—that's just the way Silva thinks."

"It's only a matter of time before McCoy is in police custody. Then the feds and local police will have to work out the details on the prosecution with the district attorney."

"I know that Phil tried to kill me, but he had a lot of issues. He was backed into a corner and acted out against me. But he didn't deserve to die like this." She closed her eyes for a second.

It tore Caleb up that Annie was upset. And to think that she was feeling such sympathy for a man that had literally tried to murder her. But that was just the type of woman Annie was. Her heart was just that big.

"I'm going to get out of here and back to work on the Silva piece of this investigation," Gabe said. Then he looked at Annie. "Keep your head up, Annie. There will be an end to all of this."

"Thanks, Gabe," she said.

Caleb followed him out and locked the door behind him. When he returned to the living room, Annie's teary eyes were open as she stared off.

He walked over and took a seat beside her. Then he wrapped his arm around her.

"Guess I'm next, huh?" she said.

"Don't talk like that."

"I have to be realistic. This is all coming to a head. He's picking us off one by one. How can I possibly get out of this?"

"We're going to figure something out. But we know who our enemies are, Annie. And sometimes that's half of the battle." He felt her shiver at his words and tightened his grip around her. "I've got you, Annie. And I'm not going to let you go."

She looked up at him with those innocent hazel eyes, and fear shot through him. A fear about his own growing feelings for her, and a fear of what would happen to him if he lost her. It was unthinkable.

"Do you have any idea how to get out of all of this?"

"That's what we're working on. The Silva piece is really tied to Doc's murder. So if we can capture McCoy and put him back into custody and get his criminal case moving along, then that would go a long way."

"I don't think Silva is just going to walk away because McCoy is apprehended. That's my fear, he's going to keep coming after me until he gets me."

"One step at a time. We are better off with McCoy in custody and being charged for Doc's murder than with McCoy out there still on his original mission to take you out. So if he is captured and the prosecution moves forward, that's a net positive for us."

"If McCoy is put on trial for Doc's murder, wouldn't you need me to testify since I was an eyewitness?"

Caleb had been dreading having this discussion. "Yes. And that's the dicey part. We'd have to work out some serious security precautions before I'd be comfortable with that. Testifying in an open courtroom presents numerous security challenges. But in the short term, let's not worry too much about that. We can only handle one obstacle at a time."

His phone rang which provided him an out of this conversation for now. He didn't want Annie to become preoccupied with a trial that may never happen.

"Yes," he answered.

He listened to what Mac had to say and then ended the call. His mind raced as he tried to take a moment to figure out how to present this to Annie. She wasn't going to like what he had to say.

"What's going on?" she asked.

"Big news."

"What?"

"McCoy has been apprehended by Atlanta PD."

"That's good right?"

"Yes." He decided it best to just go with the direct approach. "Except that they've interrogated him. And it seems like he is trying to cut a deal, and they want to talk to you to corroborate his story."

"Say what?" Annie's hazel eyes widened.

"This is all very routine. I don't know that I would've wanted to offer him a deal, but he's just a mercenary—a hired gun. The goal is to get at the decision makers in the Silva network. Not a thug."

"So you think I should just walk into the Atlanta police station and give them a statement?" she asked in a raised voice.

"Annie, I'll be by your side every step of the way. I'm not going to let anything happen to you. And this is your chance to help get justice for what happened to Doc and Phil. Isn't that what you want?"

"I thought you knew me." She paused. "That you got me. But hearing you say all of this, I can see I was dead wrong."

"Why do you say that? I'm on your side here, Annie. Talk to me." He needed to get the train back on the tracks quickly. Annie was starting to look very pale.

"Don't you get it? I don't trust the police. I don't trust anyone except you. But now I'm rethinking whether that was even such a smart idea."

He took at step toward her but she took one back. "Annie, I'm going to be there with you. I'm not going to let anyone hurt you. The criminal is in custody. The only reason they want to talk to you is so they can get more information. Like you said, you were the only eyewitness. How you lay out what happened that night will have a big impact on the terms of his plea deal. Including the fact that you watched McCoy kill Doc in cold blood."

She shook her head. "It's so much more than that, though. This could open up a whole can of worms."

He had to find a way to reassure her. "I'll be with you. Nothing bad will happen."

"You shouldn't make promises that you can't keep." As her voice started to shake, he realized he was in trouble. He'd never seen Annie this rattled before. He longed to be able to take the fear out of her eyes.

"Annie, I'm sure that after you talk to the police, then we can put this part of the nightmare behind us. Yes, McCoy will probably get a plea deal, but it's better than you having to eventually testify in trial, right?"

Her shoulders lowered a bit and she took a few deep breaths. "Maybe. But I still don't want to face interrogation. I can't go back to a situation like that. Especially not by voluntarily walking into it. Not with everything else that has happened." She stood for a moment in silence before continuing. "Here's the deal. I'll talk to the District Attorney. But that's it. Not the cops."

He wasn't sure he'd be able to swing that. "I'll do my best to make that happen."

She shook her head. "No. Please. I can't go through another interrogation. You can't imagine what it is like to be the victim, then be accused of committing a crime. I need your assurance on this."

"So this is non-negotiable?" He asked already knowing her answer.

"Exactly."

"Let me see what I can do."

"And what about the FBI mole?" she asked.

"Atlanta PD is running point right now. The FBI won't be involved in the questioning."

"And you think it's safe for me to leave here and go to this meeting?"

"We're going to have to work out the security situation. I'm not just going to take you downtown by myself that's for sure. But I feel confident that we can work something out that makes sense."

Her wounds ran even deeper than he had understood. And it floored him that, given the depth of her issues, she had allowed him into her life—and maybe into a little piece of her heart. That made him want to protect her all the more. So at that point, he decided to go out on a limb for her. "I promise you that I won't take you to the police to be interrogated."

"Thank you."

"But if it's okay with you, I would like to talk to Atlanta PD and make you coming in contingent on you speaking directly to the DA. That way, I'm the one dealing with the police, but you could still tell the prosecutor what happened that night. Would that work for you?"

"Yes," she said calmly.

"Then let me make some calls." He knew his police contacts weren't going to be crazy about these terms. But he would see what he could do.

***

Annie felt nauseous as they walked into the Fulton County District Attorney's office in downtown Atlanta. Caleb had been able to set up a meeting for her with the District Attorney—a woman named Sasha Derring.

Caleb claimed that Sasha had a sterling reputation as a straight shooter, but that didn't do anything to put Annie at ease. She wouldn't be comfortable again until she was done with this meeting and back at the safe house.

True to his word, Caleb had gotten Gabe and Kane to come with them. Between the three men, Annie felt fairly safe. She was much more afraid of coming face to face with this prosecutor. Logic told her that she shouldn't be afraid of the prosecutor, but she couldn't help but feel uneasy.

Flanked by the three men who were serving as her guards, they took the elevator up to the fifth floor. Caleb stayed beside her while Kane went to talk to the receptionist who sat behind the simple wooden desk.

"It's all going to be okay," Caleb whispered in her ear.

She appreciated his support but she still couldn't believe how he could've thought she'd be perfectly fine being interrogated by the police. How could she have been so delusional to think that they'd ever be compatible? He came at everything in his life from the viewpoint of a police officer. She couldn't fault him for who he was, but she couldn't change who she was either.

Kane walked back over to them. "The DA will be out here in a minute."

Annie steadied her breathing as she waited for what seemed like forever. When the door by the receptionist opened, a very petite woman walked out. She wore a perfectly tailored gray suit and her long dark hair was worn in a low sleek ponytail.

"You must be Annie Thomas," the woman said, offering her hand. "I'm the district attorney, Sasha Derring."

Annie shook Sasha's hand. "Nice to meet you," she said, more out of habit of being polite.

Sasha smiled at her. "We're all set up in one of our conference rooms." Sasha looked over at Caleb who was standing watch close by her side. "I would like to be able to speak with you alone, Ms. Thomas."

And that was the first time that Annie's chest tightened.

"I need to check the security of the room first." Caleb stepped forward.

"Of course. Right this way." Sasha opened up the door by the receptionist and started walking.

Kane stayed in the lobby area while Caleb and Gabe went with her down a long hallway following Sasha.

"This is just one of our regular conference rooms. Please check it out." Sasha motioned for them to enter the room.

The four of them walked into the room, and she watched closely as Caleb and Gabe had a hushed discussion. She couldn't hear what they were saying but she could take some educated guesses based on everything she'd learned since this ordeal started.

The conference room wasn't anything special. In the center of the room there was a long brown table with multiple chairs surrounding it. A couple of pictures of the city of Atlanta hung on the walls. The room was on the interior, though, so she noticed there were no windows. That might actually be a plus because that meant there was only one way in and out.

Caleb walked over to her. "This room is secure, Annie. We'll both be standing guard right outside the door. Okay?"

She was here, so she might as well just get this over with. "Yes, that's fine." There was no point in drawing this out. The sooner she started, the sooner she could get back to the safe house.

Caleb leaned down and whispered in her ear. "You have nothing to worry about. I'll be right out there by the door if you need anything."

She watched as the two men left her alone with Sasha. She noticed that there was a laptop and a notepad with a few pens on the table.

"Please have a seat, Ms. Thomas."

"You should call me Annie." There was no point in engaging in formalities.

"All right." Sasha smiled.

Sasha had a disarming quality, but Annie knew that Sasha had a job to do. And it could be that Sasha thought the best way to get the information she wanted was with a kind word and a bright smile. So Annie wasn't planning on letting down her guard. "I'm ready to get started when you are."

Sasha nodded and opened up her laptop. Annie couldn't help but notice Sasha's perfectly manicured pink nails that matched her pastel pink blouse. Not a single strand of her dark hair was out of place. Sasha seemed like everything that Annie wasn't. Annie was the definition of low maintenance, especially in her hair and makeup routine. But she didn't begrudge Sasha for taking a different approach.

"I want to get to the events surrounding Doc Perry's death. But first I have to ask you something that I was just curious about."

Annie didn't like the sound of that. "All right. What would you like to know?"

"I understand that you wanted to talk to me. That in fact, you insisted on only speaking to me. Why is it that you were so insistent about not talking to the police?"

Uh oh. That was the first sign that she was in trouble. She knew she should've never come here. She clenched her fists under the table. "Does that matter?"

"Only if you have something to hide, Annie." Sasha raised an eyebrow.

"I'm here to help. But if you don't want my help, I'm happy to leave." Annie pushed back a little from the table.

"You're free to go, but wouldn't you rather talk to me than the police?"

Sasha would have no way of knowing why she was hesitant. Annie had never been charged. She'd been a minor so there wasn't even any record of exactly what had happened as far as she knew. And there was no way that she was going to tell her about the shooting. That would only make her look like she could be guilty. So it was better to try to deflect this entire line of questioning if she could.

Sasha's dark eyes softened and she leaned forward. "Look. I've been a prosecutor for over a decade. I've seen and heard things that you probably couldn't even imagine. I can tell there's something that's bothering you. But I'm not the enemy here."

"It's complicated." And wasn't that the truth.

"If you're afraid of someone, I can make sure that you have the requisite protection."

"I really only want to talk to you. Not the police. Is that all right?"

Sasha looked at her and for a moment Annie thought she wasn't going to let her off the hook. But Sasha sighed and typed a sentence on her laptop before looking back up at her. "For the sake of moving things forward, why don't we shift gears and talk about the night of Doc Perry's murder."

"It was awful," Annie said, before she could even stop herself. She wasn't expecting to get emotional. She'd told the story multiple times, but now it somehow felt more real as she looked into Sasha's dark and discerning eyes.

"I can imagine it was. Why don't we start at the beginning and you tell me what happened step by step. You can take as much time as you need. I'm not going anywhere. So just go at your own pace."

Annie recounted the story that she had now told multiple times to different people. She didn't rush and tried to keep it as factual as possible, pushing back the wave of emotions that rolled throughout her.

"So you got in your car and just started driving?" Sasha asked.

"Yes. I feared for my life. I thought that the killer, who I now know is named McCoy, was coming after me. He was firing shots and yelling. So I thought it best to get out of there as quickly as I could."

"And didn't you have that night off of work?"

"Yes, I did."

"Why did you go there then? I'd think you wouldn't want to go to the house on your free night."

"My work is my life."

"Could you elaborate?"

How much of this did she want to reveal to her? She hated showing her vulnerability so openly but she also needed Sasha to understand. Most people probably wouldn't want to go into work on their night off. She needed to make Sasha see why she was different. "Cooking is more than just my occupation. It's a way of life for me. I don't punch a time clock. I take pride in my work. In creating new dishes and perfecting old ones."

"Which brings me back to why you were at the Perry residence on the night of the murder."

"I'd forgotten some recipe notes at the house and I really wanted to try to make a special soufflé that night as a test run. For totally new dishes, I prefer not to have the first time I serve them be the first time I've ever made them. So I went back to get the recipe notes."

"And how were things going at your job?"

"Very well. I'd held previous positions as a private chef for various families. The Perrys didn't have children in the house, as their children were older, so that made it a bit easier because I had more freedom to experiment and let them try new things. Most children have very particular tastes and wouldn't want some of the fun but more esoteric things that I would make. So I welcomed that change of pace from my previous job."

"So it sounds like you enjoyed working there."

"Yes, things were great, actually. Doc Perry really seemed to enjoy my cooking. The previous chef had been a traditionalist. I think they were getting a kick out of trying new things."

"And how were they as bosses?"

Annie wondered why Sasha cared about all of this. It definitely didn't seem relevant to the shooting. "They were very pleasant to work for. They weren't very particular and allowed me to fix whatever I wanted. They were open to new dishes and usually complimentary about my food. And if they didn't like something, then I just made a note of it and didn't make it for them again. But those were the exceptions. I've dealt with much more difficult people before."

"So you didn't have an altercation with Mr. Perry the day before he was killed?"

Wow. That came out of left field. Her stomach started to knot up at the accusatory tone to Sasha's question. "No. And in fact, I've never had any altercation with him." She didn't know where Sasha was going with this.

"I'm going to play it straight with you, Annie. Because I actually have a problem on my hands."

"What?"

"McCoy is trying to negotiate a plea deal for the murder of Phil Perry. But that deal is contingent on his testimony regarding what happened to Doc Perry."

"So are you saying that he actually confessed to both murders? Phil and Doc?"

Sasha shook her head. "No, that's the thing. McCoy admits killing Phil. The evidence against him is rock solid. But he claims that he didn't kill Doc."

"That's ridiculous. I watched him kill Doc in cold blood. I was standing right there across the room when he pulled the trigger. It's emblazoned in my memory forever."

"Annie, according to McCoy, you're the one who shot and killed Doc Perry."

CHAPTER NINE

The door to the conference room flung open and Annie rushed out of it with tears streaming down her face. Caleb ran after her, unsure of what in the world had happened.

"Annie!" He rushed down the hallway and was able to catch up with her—grabbing onto her left arm and stopping her in her tracks.

"Let me go. I need to get out of here. Now," she said with wide eyes.

"Talk to me, Annie." What could've happened to her? His own pulse sped up with concern for her.

"Only if you get me out of here."

The desperate sound in her voice let him know the gravity of the situation. But when he opened the door that led to the reception area, he saw two uniformed Atlanta police officers talking to Kane. But they had their backs turned. He made eye contact with Kane and made a split second decision based on his gut.

He grabbed onto her hand and went back down the hall toward the stairwell. "This way," he told her.

He felt her shaking as he gripped onto her tighter. This was all his fault. Something had gone wrong and he had no idea what had happened. Only that now he had a terrified, shaky Annie in his arms. He'd given his word to her that he wasn't going to put her in front of the police. He intended to keep that promise no matter what the cost.

They ran quickly down the stairwell but it wasn't long before Gabe caught up with them.

"This way," Gabe said.

Once they hit the first floor and exited the building, his heart started to race even more. Annie was keeping up as they ran down the street and toward the parking garage.

"We need to get to the car," Caleb said. His immediate concern was Annie's safety and keeping her away from the police.

Gabe looked over his shoulder. "I don't see anyone tailing us but we should move."

Less than a minute later, they were in the car with Gabe driving and Caleb in the backseat trying to console Annie. But she wasn't looking good. He needed to figure out what happened and quickly, because he was operating in the dark. And that wasn't how he liked to operate.

"Annie, please talk to me. We need to understand what happened in there."

She didn't respond for a couple of minutes. He knew that he needed to give her some time to pull herself together. But in the meantime, he started scenario building in his head, trying to figure out what could have gone wrong in that room.

Then she looked up into his eyes, clearly shell shocked. "McCoy told the police that I'm the one who killed Doc. That I'm a murderer!"

Whoa. Now that was ludicrous. "Are you sure?"

"Certain."

"Wait a minute," Gabe said. "Let's think about it. McCoy could cut himself a deal *and* finish his assignment if he pins the murder on Annie. He knew he would have to admit he killed Phil, but then this way he is able to take out Annie too by pointing the finger at her."

"I never imagined that he would come up with something so far-fetched," Caleb said. He started questioning whether he was losing his edge. It bothered him that this turn of events didn't even pop up on his radar. And now Annie was being tormented because of it.

"I told you I didn't want to go down there," she said. "And this is exactly why."

Her words were like a punch to the gut. The last thing he had wanted was for her to be hurt. "I'm sorry that I pushed you, but we're still going to make this right. McCoy won't get away with this."

"You still don't understand, do you? You say it's far-fetched, but to a hungry prosecutor and a police department I don't know or trust, they would jump on something like this." Her voice was strained as she spoke.

"Tell me what happened in there with the DA," Caleb said. "We need to hear everything."

"I told my side of the story. The same thing you've heard now a million times. Then she started to go down a completely different path. She asked if I was happy with my job. I told her I was. Then she asked if I had an altercation with Doc. Of course, I told her no to that, too. I was really confused. I wasn't sure why she was asking those questions because I'd never had any trouble while working at the Perrys' house. And I surely didn't ever have any type of altercation with Doc. We haven't ever had an argument." She paused and looked directly at him. "Then that's when she dropped the bomb that McCoy had told the police that I was actually the one who killed Doc. I was in such shock that I just bolted from the room. I couldn't fathom what was happening. It was like my nightmare was playing out right there in front of me. I reacted the only way I could at the moment."

Gabe glanced back at them in the rearview mirror. "But given everything you've just said, it doesn't sound like she was accusing you. More like asking to get your side of the story. You don't know that Sasha was going to put any credence into McCoy's accusation. But if he did make that allegation against you, then it was up to her to ask and see how you responded."

"Then why were there police officers waiting for me in the lobby?" she asked. "If she was going to give me a fair shake, she shouldn't have called in the cops for a surprise attack."

"Good point," Caleb said. "But maybe we're overreacting. It may have just been a precaution. We haven't talked to Kane. We don't know that they were there for you."

"I'm not willing to risk it. This whole thing just went from bad to worse. I'm not the criminal here and yet I feel like they're treating me like one."

"I know you two aren't going to like this," Gabe said. "But running makes you look like you have something to hide. We could try to contact Sasha and attempt to get this worked out. It's a prosecutor's job to get to the truth. She wouldn't have any reason to try to pin a murder on you that you didn't commit. Every interaction I've ever had with her has led me to believe that she's one of the good guys."

"But we don't know one hundred percent that she's clean," Caleb added. "We made the assumption going in that she was or we would've never gone. But the fact that she's even entertaining a criminal's story is a problem for me. Let's get back to the safe house and regroup." Caleb looked out the back window again. "It doesn't look like we've been pursued at this point."

"Doesn't mean they won't be coming," she said.

"All the more reason to get back to the safe house," Caleb replied.

"Uh oh," Gabe said. "May have spoke too soon. A dark SUV has been behind us for a couple of blocks."

"If it was the police, wouldn't they be in a police car?" Annie asked.

"More than likely yes. But there are unmarked cars," Caleb said. He turned and looked at what Gabe had pointed out. "But the bigger problem is if it isn't the police."

"I'm going to lose them. Hang on you two," Gabe said.

***

Annie tried to focus on the immediate threat and not get sucked back into the abyss of what had just taken place at the prosecutor's office. Gabe's evasive driving was proving to be quite a wild ride. But he seemed like a highly skilled driver, despite the erratic moves.

Caleb squeezed her hand as Gabe took another erratic turn. The combination of Gabe's driving skills and the Atlanta traffic might play into their favor.

"You see them?" Gabe asked.

Caleb answered. "No. I think we may have shaken them."

"Gabe, watch out!" she yelled when she saw an oncoming truck crossing the center line.

He jerked the wheel hard to the right. They hit the curb, but kept on going. "I'm getting on the freeway after the next block. Hang on."

When they entered the freeway, she let out a breath. They could go much faster on the highway, and she didn't feel as constrained by the city streets and traffic. It was like she could actually take a few full breaths without fearing hyperventilating.

"We need to make sure we're not being followed before we can go to the safe house," Gabe said.

"Roger that," Caleb said. "I've got eyes back here. Nothing so far."

Annie stayed quiet for the next half an hour as they drove around trying to make sure they'd lost their tail. Though she wasn't speaking, she was definitely thinking.

She felt since Caleb was a police officer himself, he couldn't look at the situation objectively. There was no way she was going to voluntarily go back to the police after what Sasha had confronted her with. And even though Sasha seemed like a nice enough person, that didn't mean Annie trusted her. Who could she trust?

Caleb had pushed her into going to the meeting, and could she really blame him? He saw everything through the law enforcement lens. Another reason why the two of them had no business being together. They'd always look at things differently. This wasn't like one person wanting cheese pizza and the other wanting pepperoni. No, this was a piece of her that went to the very core of who she was. She couldn't go back in time and change the events of her past. And she couldn't just close her eyes and pretend like those things hadn't happened to her.

She needed a way out of this quickly, because she had a sinking feeling that after all was said and done, both Caleb and Gabe would end up wanting her to go back and talk to the police and Sasha. But that was because they based their beliefs on the assumption that all law enforcement was good. She'd lived through a different reality.

Annie was glad when they pulled back up into the driveway at the safe house. She really wanted some time away from the guys to decompress.

"Gabe, please go do a security sweep," Caleb said. "I'll stay here with Annie until you give us the all clear."

"Be back in a few." Gabe got out of the car and started walking toward the safe house.

Caleb looked at her. "Annie, I know you're upset. And you have every right to be. I get that you're angry and frustrated, and probably a lot of other things right now too."

"I don't think you can fully appreciate where I'm coming from." There was no point in sugar coating her feelings. "You and I come from such different places based on all of our personal experiences. You did what you thought was right, and I don't hold you personally responsible. I hold myself responsible for going down a road I never wanted to in the first place. And ..."

"Yes?"

"I need to be clear with you. I'm not going to turn myself over to the police. No matter what you say or what assurances you make me. I've struggled with my past for over a decade and this is like reliving the pain I went through all over again. It's been bad enough with everything else that has happened, but this is about to put me at the breaking point."

"Annie," he said in a strained voice. "Haven't I shown you that I'm willing to do anything and everything to defend you? There's no way I would want to put you in harm's way."

"Not on purpose. I get that. But you believe that everyone's intentions are pure, and that's not the case."

He put his hand on her knee. "I'm frustrated just like you are."

"But you're not the one being accused of murder."

"We're going to clear your name of any alleged wrongdoing. McCoy is just desperate and trying to make any play that he can."

"I want to believe that, I really do. But that is really hard." She tried to gather up her thoughts. She looked up and saw Gabe running out of the front door and yelling.

"Something's wrong," she said.

Caleb jumped into the front seat just as Gabe slid into the passenger side.

"Floor it!" Gabe said. "Go, go, go!"

Caleb hit the gas and they backed out of the driveway with a loud screeching sound just as the explosion happened. The safe house blew up into a ball of bright orange fire with huge plumes of black smoke.

She sat in shock staring out the back window as Caleb sped down the neighborhood road.

"How did this happen?" Caleb asked in a raised voice.

"We've been compromised," Gabe responded.

"But how?" Caleb asked.

"I don't know. We had such a tight circle of those who knew we were at the DEA safe house."

"You saw the device?"

"Yes. It was state of the art. Not a hack job."

"Call Kane," Caleb told Gabe.

"This was his safe house. How do we know that he isn't the one who planted the bomb?" she asked.

"I know Kane. This wasn't his doing," Gabe replied. He put his phone on speaker. "Kane, it's Gabe."

"You all ran out of the office. What happened back there?" Kane asked.

"We've got bigger problems than the prosecutor and police. The DEA safe house just went up in smoke. We all could've been killed."

"What do you mean?" Kane asked.

"I'm talking about a bomb."

"What type of device?"

"A very professionally made one."

"This is crazy. I thought that DEA location would've been completely secure. And we've kept those who knew to a very few people. So I'm not sure how this could've happened."

"But now we have to keep it even tighter. We need options," Caleb said.

"I've got my own personal safe house. It's totally off the grid and not associated with any official DEA ops. I'll send you the address. Let's meet there."

She couldn't wait and needed to ask him about the other issue in the forefront of her mind. "What happened with the police?"

"They were there to question you. But I figured something went sideways with the DA, so I stalled them as long as I could. Then she came out a couple of minutes later and I got out of there before they could start questioning me."

"Okay. Text us the address and we'll meet you there," Gabe said as he ended the call.

"What are we going to do?" she asked quietly.

"Pray," Caleb said.

And that's just what she did. All the way to the new safe house while Gabe and Caleb tried to talk about how this all could've happened and how they were going to move forward.

When they arrived at the new safe house, Annie went directly to the kitchen to make a much needed pot of coffee. She was surrounded by Caleb, Gabe, and Kane. The men were debating next steps. She intended to provide her opinion once they had viable ideas on the table. Right now nothing seemed very realistic—or safe. They were throwing out all kinds of plans that seemed far-fetched.

"So what about getting out of Georgia?" Gabe asked. "Hitting the road and starting to drive to get away from here? Just try to remove Annie from the entire situation."

"We'd have to think about what locations could make sense. We definitely wouldn't want to go to Florida," Caleb said.

"Why not?" Annie asked. That got her attention since she was originally from Florida.

"We need to steer clear. Silva's cousin Damon Vaughn runs the Florida operations and he's rumored to be just as ruthless as Silva," Gabe said. "That would be trading one problem for another."

Annie dropped the coffee mug, and it shattered into a million tiny pieces onto the floor. The world felt like it was closing in all around here. She tried to take a breath, but no air filled her lungs.

"Annie, are you all right?" Caleb asked.

"No."

"Tell me what's wrong."

"Everything."

CHAPTER TEN

Annie didn't feel like she was standing on solid ground. As the room started to spin, she willed herself to stay focused. *Dear Lord, give me strength.*

Kane was on one side of her and Caleb on the other. She realized they were both holding onto her. Had she almost fainted?

"We've got you, Annie," Caleb said. His deep voice was soothing and calm. His grip on her right arm was a steadying force in her time of need.

She was safe. She had to remind herself that. But this revelation changed everything. All of a sudden she realized why things had gotten so bad. "I need to tell you all something."

"Why don't we sit down and then we can talk about it," Gabe suggested.

Annie nodded, thinking that was a good idea. Because if she didn't sit, she didn't know how much longer she could stand. "I know now that this isn't just about me witnessing Doc's murder."

"What else could there be?" Caleb asked.

Could she even form the words? She needed to put it all out there. This would put everything into a different perspective. "Caleb, remember when I told you about my mom's boyfriend. The man I shot in self defense when I was seventeen?"

He narrowed his eyebrows. "Yeah. But what does that have to do with this?"

She took a deep breath. "That man's name was Damon Vaughn."

Caleb let out a low whistle and looked over at Gabe and then back at her. "No way that's a coincidence. And the Florida connection is there. You grew up in South Florida, right, Annie?"

"Yes. South Florida."

"Can we back up for a second. I'm completely lost," Kane said. "Can someone fill me in so I know what we're talking about."

Annie took a minute and retold the story about what had happened to her. How she had shot Damon in self-defense when she was seventeen. It was actually easier retelling it than it had been the first time to Caleb. Kane was also able to pull up a picture of Damon on his phone—confirming her worst nightmares. That it was the same man from her troubled past. There was no doubt in her mind, as she stared into his eyes, that this was the same man.

"That would explain a lot," Gabe said. "Like why Silva has put so much time and resources into finding you. Initially, you were just one of his regular loose ends. But I bet when he put out the word to his network, and Vaughn was clued in, then that's when he decided to really go after you."

"And now he's using this as an opportunity for revenge," Caleb added.

Hearing them play the theory out made it even more real for her. And more terrifying. "So how does this impact the plan?"

"Everyone stays put for tonight. The only people that know the location of this place are the people in the house right now," Kane said. "I suggest you don't even clue in your family, Caleb. That way we can ensure there are absolutely no leaks."

"Agreed. For now. It's radio silence," Caleb said.

"Kane and I should start doing some leg work on the Vaughn angle now that we have these new facts," Gabe said. "One or both of us will be back soon with more supplies and any updates."

***

The next morning Caleb needed to get his head on straight. The information had been coming at him fast and furious. He couldn't believe how troublesome the connection between Damon Vaughn and Annie was. Just when he thought things couldn't get any more dangerous for Annie. *Lord, I need Your help. I want to be able to defend and protect Annie. But there are so many threats and I'm just one man.*

He felt like their backs were up against the wall, and how they responded could change everything. There was a knock at the door and he jumped up from his seat at the kitchen table. He walked over to the front door and looked through the peephole. He let out a breath. Gabe and Hope were standing on the other side.

He opened the door. "Come on in."

Gabe looked at him. "I know we said keep the circle tight, but I thought that given the circumstances Hope could talk to Annie about what happened with Sasha."

"That's a great idea," Caleb said. Given Hope's experience as an attorney, she might be able to provide some support to Annie that he wasn't able to give. "She's still upstairs. She hasn't come down yet this morning. Honestly, I don't think she really wants to talk to me right now."

"Let me see what I can do. I'll go up to see Annie and let you guys talk." Hope smiled at him and patted him on the shoulder. "It's going to be okay, Caleb. We're going to shut down these guys before they can do more harm." Hope left the two of them in the living room and headed up to find Annie, leaving him alone with Gabe.

"Is she freaked out over the bomb?" Caleb asked him.

"She knows that I have a high risk career. But of course she was worried. And not just for me, for all of us."

"I'm sorry to have brought you into this." He was putting his best friend in harm's way. And he didn't like that one bit.

"I know you'd be there for me in the same way in a heartbeat. Just like you've been in the past. Don't worry about me. I've got your back," Gabe said.

"Thanks, man."

"Kane and I have been working most of the night trying to pull together files for intel on Vaughn. Everything we know about Damon Vaughn." Caleb handed him over a large manila envelope. "It should give you some more insight into this guy. But from what I've read, I'm telling you it's not pretty."

"Let me guess. He's just as bad as Silva?"

Gabe nodded. "If not worse. But Silva currently has a tighter grip on controlling the entire organization. I spoke to Kane again a few minutes ago, and there have actually been rumblings that Vaughn wants to run the whole show one day."

"A coup?" Caleb asked.

"Maybe. But according to intel, nothing is imminent. Maybe Vaughn is just hoping for a peaceful transition. Silva's got almost twenty years on him."

"Are you comfortable with Kane and this entire DEA angle?" Caleb now felt it was his job to question everything and everyone. He couldn't afford to be blindsided again.

"Yes. I know that Kane's the real deal. He won't jeopardize Annie's safety."

"Given that we're completely off the grid at the moment. Do you think Mike is up for the task of holding down the fort in Maxwell?"

"Sure. I know he's a little cranky, but he knows the ins and outs of Maxwell better than any of us. Better be careful or he won't want to give the power back to you upon your return."

Caleb couldn't help but laugh. "Yeah. I know. We had a rough patch when I started as chief, but he's all good now. He's actually been very supportive for the past year. He's got his eye toward retirement in a couple of years anyway."

"Once Hope finishes up with Annie, I'm going to go and run down a few more things I wanted to check out on Vaughn."

"Sounds like a plan."

"How do you think Annie's doing?"

"She's upset about Vaughn for sure. But she doesn't even realize how strong she is. And she's clearly still mad about what happened with Sasha."

"That's why I thought bringing Hope over might help. I knew Annie was distressed after the meeting with Sasha. And rightfully so."

"And you know one thing that's been bothering me?"

"What?"

"Why was Atlanta PD there at Sasha's office?"

"Maybe Sasha told them when the interview was taking place with Annie and they wanted to play ball?"

"But I specifically had an agreement with her, no cops," Caleb said. "I would like to think that a prosecutor wouldn't lie like that."

"You're right. Her setting up Annie would be totally inconsistent with her sterling reputation."

"We already know that there is most likely someone in the FBI on Silva's payroll. But even if there is an FBI mole, how would they have known about the timing of the interview?"

"Just another reason for us to be extra cautious."

***

Annie sat on the edge of the bed beside Hope. Hope wasn't the person Annie had expected when she'd heard the knock on the bedroom door. But, man, was she glad to see her.

"When Gabe told me all that had happened, I thought it would be good to come and have a chat with you. I can help give you the lawyer perspective on all of this." She paused. "But even more importantly than that, I know what it's like to need a friend in a rough time. And as great as the guys are, sometimes they just don't get it."

Annie was grateful for Hope reaching out. Even though she knew Hope couldn't solve any of her problems with Sasha or the Atlanta PD, just being there and listening was important. "Sasha seemed inherently suspicious of everything I was saying. Like all of a sudden I was under a microscope and she was trying her best to pick me apart piece by piece."

"That's just the lawyer talking. When a lawyer is conducting an interview—any interview—if they are any good at their job, they will ask probing questions, because even if a detail or fact seems insignificant in your mind, it could have a legal implication for the case. I wouldn't take her pushing you on questions as her not believing you. Sometimes lawyers push just to confirm that the witness is truthful, that their story is consistent and could hold up in court."

"I think if it would just have been that, then maybe I would've been okay. But when she told me that McCoy had pointed the finger at me for Doc's murder, it just sent me over the edge. I totally lost it. I know the guys think I'm totally crazy, but I couldn't help it."

"As your friend, I can totally sympathize, and I'm sure the guys don't think you're crazy. If anything, they think that you're amazing for being able to handle every single thing that has been thrown at you. I can speak from experience, though, I don't want you to feel like Sasha was personally attacking you. She was just doing her job. Seeing how you reacted to his allegation was part of her legal analysis. During the interview every question she asked was to help gain information and evaluate your credibility.

After she gets all the facts from all the people involved, she'll make her decision about who she believes is telling the truth. And I know I haven't known you for that long, Annie, but you present yourself as an honest person. You make eye contact when you talk to people, you speak clearly, you answer questions with real answers not the run around. Sasha is a top notch prosecutor. I have no doubt that she will get to the truth—and that will include McCoy being prosecuted and you being a witness—not a suspect."

"Thank you for saying all of that."

"I wanted to say it because I believe it's true and that it's helpful for you to hear my take on things, but I'm also here to listen to you vent. Not as a lawyer, but as a friend. So lay it on me." Hope laughed.

Annie almost got teary at Hope's kind words. If she got through all of this alive, she prayed that she and Hope could stay friends. "I'm running out of steam, and I felt like Caleb didn't really get why I was so upset. He and I come from such different worlds. He grew up in a stable home with loving parents and siblings. I was an only child with a drug addicted mother."

"Your upbringing shaped you, Annie. No doubt about it. But it doesn't have to define you. It seems to me that you've done really well for yourself, and you're used to doing things on your own. Believe me—I was the same way. You and I are a lot alike."

"You think so?"

"Yes. I grew up very poor. There were many days when I didn't know if I'd have anything for dinner. That impacted me so much, and on top of that, or maybe as a result of that, my mom was an alcoholic. She chose to spend what little money there was on booze instead of food."

"Really?" Annie asked. "I would've never thought that you'd had a tough childhood. You're so put together."

"Far from it. At least for many years. Oh, I've had some difficult times in my life. I had a career plan. I threw all of my time and energy into law school, into getting a job at a top New York law firm. I thought that if I got to the top of the firm, it would make me more than I was. But I realized that I was fooling myself. I was looking for worth in all the wrong places. Growing in my faith really helped me become the woman I am today. And honestly, Gabe helped me a lot too. His love for me made me realize that I was okay just the way I was. And that all the struggles I went through made me a unique person who had truly lived life."

"Sounds like the two of you have something very special. Can I ask you something?"

"Sure," Hope said.

"What made you take the leap with Gabe?"

"I was scared initially because I felt like I had to give up so much to be with him. But then I realized I wasn't giving up things that mattered, that what was important was the love I had for him. He was willing to leave Maxwell and come to New York with me, but I didn't want to go back to that life. I wanted to start a new life in Maxwell. One that didn't revolve around defining my worth over the number of hours I billed at the firm."

"Well, my career is obviously different, but I can relate. I throw myself into my work, and I know that I use it as an escape. When I'm in the kitchen the rest of my problems don't invade that space. It's my safe zone."

"You don't have to give up what you love doing, Annie. It's just a matter of perspective and not running from the very good things that might be right within your grasp."

"And not using being a chef as a crutch or an excuse not to live out fully the rest of my life." Annie paused. "I'm not going to lie. It all sounds good, but it's easier said than done. All I can do is take it one step at a time."

"I can see it in the way you look at Caleb. You care for him. Don't let what happened to you before make you miss out on the opportunity for a life changing relationship."

She nodded and wondered if she was capable of following Hope's advice.

"Caleb is such a good man. And I can tell you from what Gabe has told me, Caleb hasn't been in a serious relationship since before he left for the military. So the fact that he's so interested in you shows that this is special. That you're special to him."

"Thanks for everything, Hope. I wish it would've been under different circumstances, but I'm really enjoying getting to know you."

"That goes both ways." Hope looked down at her watch. "I better go see if Gabe is ready to go. I know he said he had to do some more investigating."

"Thank you again, Hope. For everything."

As Hope left the room, Annie thanked God for sending a much needed friend into her life.

***

Caleb locked the door after Gabe and Hope left, just as Annie was coming down the stairs. She looked a little tired, but still beautiful to him. He would do anything to take away the hurt he knew she was facing.

"How did you sleep?" he asked.

"I've had better nights," she said. "But it was nice being able to see Hope again."

"I'm sorry about your night, but I'm glad Hope came over too. She has a lot of first hand experience living through dangerous times." Caleb pointed to the coffee table. "Gabe dropped off a file on Vaughn. I'm going to do the deep dive and get totally up to speed on everything law enforcement knows about him."

"Okay. Then we should start." Annie walked over to the coffee table. "Let's take a look at what's in Damon's file."

"I don't know if that is such a good idea for you, Annie." He was worried of what might be in the file. "I think I should take a look first."

"After all I've been through, do you really think that it's necessary to try and shield me from the truth?"

He was taken aback by her visceral response. "The last thing I want to do is hurt you. Since I haven't read the file, I can't guarantee what we'll find in there."

"I can handle it."

He reached down and picked up the file and prayed that this was the right thing to do.

* * *

Annie could sense Caleb's hesitation as he opened the large manila folder that contained the information on the man that had wrecked her life. She needed to do this. Not just for the sake of the investigation and trying to secure her safety, but because she needed to prove to herself that she wasn't the scared and confused seventeen year old girl anymore. No, she was so much stronger now and she could beat this. Or at least that's what she kept telling herself.

"Caleb, I already lived through the worst of this when I was seventeen."

"But I know good and well that a trigger to a traumatic event can really have an impact on someone."

What was he talking about? It sounded like he was speaking from personal experience. Maybe the death of his parents? "I promise you. I can do this. We already know that Damon Vaughn is not a good person."

He reached out and grabbed onto her hand. "Annie, do you trust me?"

She paused, conflicted between what she thought she should feel and what she was actually feeling. Her mind told her that she should never trust anyone ever again—and certainly not a man in law enforcement. But her heart told her that Caleb was loyal and would stay true to his word. In the end, she knew how she had to respond. "Yes, I do."

"Let's do this together then."

The next couple of hours they waded through pages and pages of documents about Damon Vaughn. Everything from his troubled youth to his current illegal activities. His familial connection to Silva on his mother's side and an obvious quest for more power that had been building over the years. From reading all the intel that had been gathered, it was clear that Damon was every bit as dangerous now as he was a decade ago when he had attacked her. The only difference is that now he was even more of a threat because he actually had become a power player in the Silva organization. Back when Damon had dated her mother, he was still an up and comer.

"This is all interesting reading, but how does any of this help me get out of this mess?" she asked.

"Vaughn's connection to you and Silva provides the motive for McCoy to lie about you killing Doc. We've got to take this to Sasha."

"How do you know that you can trust her?"

"I don't know for sure, but we need to clear your name. We can't afford to have the police looking for you in addition to Silva and Vaughn trying to track you down."

"I don't feel comfortable going down there to Sasha's office again."

"No, that wouldn't be the plan. First, we'll call her. Try to gauge where she's at. Then determine after she hears this information whether it would be appropriate to meet. Gabe said that Sasha has a very strong reputation as being ethical and being fair. I see no reason to think that she'd be out to get you."

"Unless Silva has gotten to her, too."

"Not everyone is on Silva's payroll."

"But we know that there are at least some people in law enforcement who are." She let out a breath. "Honestly, I feel like I'm reliving the nightmare of my past."

"The truth is on your side, Annie. It was back then and it still is today. Sasha will be able to see that." He reached out and took her hand in his. "I'd like to make that call. But before we do, I could tell that you were very upset about what happened at the DA's office."

"We've been over this already." The thing was, that there was nothing Caleb could say to change the circumstances. Her point of view was shaped by her experiences just like his was. "I don't feel like expending energy that neither one of us has arguing over our differences."

"Whoa." He squeezed onto her hand. "How did we get from me making a mistake to us having differences?"

"Caleb, I appreciate all you're doing for me. You've saved my life countless times. You've proven to be a friend I could trust when there was no one to turn to. But as far as there being something more than friendship between us, I don't see how we can find common ground. Your whole life revolves around law enforcement. You have a completely normal and loving family. A well-adjusted way of life. And then you have me, who has never had any of that."

"I think you're looking at this all wrong." His blue eyes locked onto hers. "Yes, you went through a terrible tragedy when you were seventeen. And it caused you a lot of heartache and pain. But I know what it's like to live in the past. It will eat at you from the inside out. You need to try to find a pathway forward."

"Are you talking about the death of your parents?"

"That definitely impacted me. Losing them was heartbreaking. But it's more than just the loss of my parents that has made me the man I am today."

"You're talking about what you experienced in the military." He'd alluded to it before, but she didn't have any specifics.

"Yes. And I'd like to tell you about it."

***

Caleb hadn't discussed exactly what had happened in Afghanistan with anyone. But as he stared into Annie's eyes and saw the pain she was going through and the struggles she was facing, it made him think that maybe if he shared his experience with her, that it could provide some small level of healing to them both.

"What happened?" she asked.

"I've told you before that I was in the military, and that I did special ops. It's a bit more than that. I was on a SEAL team."

"You were a Navy SEAL?" Her eyes widened.

"Once a SEAL, always a SEAL. But yes. My team was on a special high value target mission in Afghanistan hunting down some really bad men. I can't discuss the actual details of the operation because that's still classified. But..." As he started to continue the story, he wondered for a moment if he would actually be able to get the words out.

She grabbed onto his other hand, now holding them both. "Take your time. It's not like I'm going anywhere." She gave him a slight smile, trying to encourage him.

"One second everything was fine. The next, it was complete chaos. We were ambushed. I was with one other SEAL and we were cut off from the rest of our team."

"Oh no," she said.

"And to make matters worse, it had been my idea for the two of us to go ahead and do some advanced recon. I didn't know that we were walking into a trap."

"There's no way you could've known that, Caleb. You made the best decision you could at the time."

"And that decision—the decision I made as the leader of the Team—that decision got my fellow SEAL killed."

She flinched. "I am so sorry."

"I saw the bullets riddle his body. I watched him take his last breath." He fought back tears as the pain seemed as real as it was that day years ago. "But somehow, someway, I survived. I pulled his body out of the line of fire when the rest of my team arrived to help. But it was too late. He was gone. And it was all because I'd made the decision for the two of us to go ahead of the rest of the team."

Annie's eyes were filled with tears, and she kept her grip on his hands. "I can't even imagine."

"I was never the same after that. A part of me died out there in the mountains of Afghanistan that day. A piece of me that I'll never get back. So when I tell you I can empathize with what you went through, I believe that I can. And I went through a really dark period after that. I didn't know why God had spared me and taken my friend. A man who in my opinion was a much better man than I'll ever be. I questioned everything. I isolated myself from everyone—my SEAL buddies, my family." He paused for a moment and figured if he was being brutally honest he should just put it all out there. "I even wondered if my life was worth living."

"How did you get through it?"

"I'll never get over it, Annie. But with God's help, I have been able to live with it. I couldn't do it on my own. By myself, I was a complete wreck. Depressed, lonely, angry. I was so mad at everything—mostly at myself. One day I just lost it and fell to my knees in prayer. It wasn't an immediate solution. But day by day, I got stronger. I was able to use the emotions I had and channel them into something positive. Make no mistake though, I'm forever changed because of what happened. So when you talk about being damaged, Annie, I'm damaged, too. I'm just a man who has a past full of nightmares, but who is living each day by the grace of God."

Tears were falling down Annie's face. "I don't even know what to say."

"I haven't ever told anyone else what I just told you."

She tilted her head to the side. "Then why me?"

"Because you matter to me, Annie. Like no other woman ever has."

"You could do so much better than me, Caleb."

He shook his head. "No. I like you just the way you are. The way I see it, we're perfectly matched."

"Even with all my issues?"

"Your issues make you who you are. I'm not looking for perfection. I'm looking for a real connection. And I believe that you feel it between us, too. Something strong and real."

"I do. But..."

He lifted his finger to her lips to stop her. "No buts. Not right now."

She nodded and looked up at him. And he could see in her eyes that she felt something for him as well. He leaned down and kissed her gently, realizing he had already given this woman his heart.

***

The next day Annie sat anxiously waiting for him to make the call to Sasha. Annie was still reeling from what Caleb had told her yesterday. He'd opened up to her in a way that he hadn't with anyone else. And she knew that meant something.

But she was still scared to death about her own feelings. Even if he said that he accepted her as she was, did he really know what that would entail? And yes, he had a traumatic past, too, but there was a big difference. He was stronger than she was. He had a rough time and he came through it on the other side. She didn't know if she ever would fully be the woman she wanted to be.

She was always bouncing back to her childhood. The lack of love and security. The lack of a father. A mother with addiction issues. And that was on top of the entire shooting episode. She'd survived this long because she insulated herself from others. She didn't rely upon anyone else for anything. Her way of self-sufficiency was how she managed.

But now she had this man in her life who was wanting more. Wanting her to step out of the shadows of her past. Even if she wanted to, could she?

"You ready to do this?" Caleb asked.

"Not really, but I realize we don't have much of an alternative." And that was true. She was boxed into a corner. After having slept on it, she realized her best option was to try to get on the good side of the prosecutor. And pray that Sasha wasn't bought off by Silva. Hope's insight had also provided her a small measure of comfort that talking to Sasha was the best option.

He dialed Sasha's direct office line on speaker and they waited.

"This is Sasha Derring," she answered.

"Sasha, this is Caleb Winters and Annie Thomas."

"Ah. I was hoping that I would hear from you. Annie, I'm so sorry that things got a little out of control when we met. That was never my intention. I really want to finish our discussion."

"That's why we're calling," he said. "Annie filled me in on what McCoy's accusation was, and we have some information about why he would have a motivation to lie about Annie."

"All right. I'm listening," Sasha said.

"I'll let Annie tell you," he said.

She wanted to be able to provide the information to Sasha herself. "Sasha, when I was seventeen I shot my mom's boyfriend in self defense. Did you know that?"

"No. I didn't."

"I just recently found out that the man I shot, Damon Vaughn, is Tim Silva's cousin."

"He runs the Florida part of the Silva enterprise," Caleb added.

"Well, that's an interesting turn of events," Sasha said.

"We believe that Silva has targeted Annie not just because she witnessed McCoy shoot and kill Doc Perry, but because his cousin Vaughn wants revenge."

Annie realized she was holding her breath as she waited to hear Sasha's reaction.

"And you're implying that McCoy would lie about Annie killing Doc because he's gotten the order to do so from Silva or Vaughn."

"Exactly," Caleb said. "Annie isn't a killer. She's an upstanding citizen. It's her word versus a mercenary hit man who has already confessed to killing Phil Perry."

Sasha sighed loudly. "If you two hadn't run out the other day, I would've told you myself that I didn't think there was merit to McCoy's allegation. But the police can't just ignore his statements."

"I don't trust the police," Annie said. "We don't know who Silva has in his back pocket."

"Annie's right. We have narrowly escaped with our lives multiple times now. We're coming to you because we don't believe that Silva has influence over you. But at this point, I no longer feel confident I can say the same thing about the Atlanta police or the FBI."

"I understand your fears," Sasha said. "Let me do some digging on my end including interviewing McCoy again. I appreciate you reaching out. But know that I can't control the actions of the Atlanta police."

"Understood. Thanks." He hung up the phone and looked at her.

"Do you think she believes me?" she asked.

"I do. She's a smart prosecutor. She knows better than to believe a totally concocted story. It's just a matter, like she said, that the police have different obligations and interests. They like to question everyone."

A loud knock on the door had her jumping.

"It's okay," he said. "I'm sure it's one of the guys."

She trailed him as he went to open the door.

Mac walked in the door.

"How did you find us?" Caleb asked. "No offense, but we were supposed to be completely off the grid."

"Listen to me, bro. We've got a problem."

"Come on in and tell me what's going on." They walked into the living room.

Mac turned and looked at Caleb. "Gabby's missing."

CHAPTER ELEVEN

Caleb thought he heard his brother wrong. "Missing? What do you mean?"

"She's gone dark. Completely. No contact from her cell. I went to her apartment and checked your house. She's nowhere to be found."

Caleb started thinking. A bad feeling swelled through his gut. "Did Gabby talk to you about Silva's drug operations in Maxwell?"

"No. Not a word. Was she supposed to?" Mac asked.

"This is all my fault," Annie said. "I bet she was trying to help us."

"This isn't your fault, Annie," he responded.

Mac crossed his arms. "Please fill me in on what you're talking about."

Caleb could tell by the look on his brother's face, that Mac wasn't going to like what he had to tell him. "Gabby called me and told me that Silva had moved some drug ops into Maxwell. Specifically, she said there was some type of warehouse she wanted to investigate."

"What? And you encouraged her?" Mac asked in a raised voice.

"Absolutely not. Just the opposite. I told her to step back. That things had gotten far too dangerous."

"And she promised she would," Annie added. "I heard her say that she would."

"Well, it looks like she didn't. And now she's gone." Mac started pacing back and forth.

"Maybe she's on another job," Caleb said.

"And not answering her phone or email? No way," Mac said. "We've always stayed in contact regardless of the job. You know that's how we operate."

"Then we need to consider that this is Silva's doing." Caleb didn't want to say the words because then that made it seem more real. But he didn't see any other alternative that made sense given all the facts.

"He's trying to get to you, to me through your sister. Once again, this is my fault," Annie said. "What can I do? We've got to find her."

"Let's think this through," Caleb said. They needed all the help they could get, as they were fighting this battle on multiple fronts. The thought of Silva having his little sister made him sick. And angry. But getting mad wasn't going to solve their problem. No, he had to act smart right now. Gabby's life might depend on it.

"I'm going to go start the search for her. I need to find this warehouse you're talking about. What if they're holding her there?" Mac asked. "Any idea where it could be?"

Caleb was trying to keep his cool because Mac was close to losing it. "Just that it was supposed to be in Maxwell. Contact Mike. He offered to keep an eye out for her. Maybe he's seen something that can give us some leads on her whereabouts. Also bring Gabe in and get him to help you. I can't leave Annie alone here."

Mac nodded. "Yeah, we can use all the help we can get. Bro, if something happens to Gabby, I don't know what I'll do."

"We can't think like that right now. Gabby's strong and resourceful. We need to stay positive and think clearly if we want to do our best to help her."

"I'll be fine if you need to go, Caleb." Annie stepped forward. "No one knows that we're here."

"Absolutely not. I'm not going to leave you here by yourself. We don't have any guarantee that this location is one hundred percent secure."

Annie took a step toward him. "Well, then take me with you and I can help."

Caleb shook his head. "Annie, taking you into the unknown is also not an option at this point. We don't need more problems than we already have."

"Armed with this intel about the storage facility in Maxwell that she told you about, I'm going to go back to town and start searching for her. I'll keep you updated. I don't want to waste any time. Each minute could matter," Mac said. He walked toward the door. "I'll call Gabe from the road."

"Keep me posted," he replied.

Once Mac closed the door and left, he turned around and faced Annie.

"I'm so sorry. This is my fault. The only reason she was doing any work related to Silva was because of me."

"No, Annie. The responsibility lies with Silva, not you. He's the criminal here."

"You need to be out there looking for Gabby. Not here baby-sitting me. She's your sister, Caleb. She needs you right now, and I don't want to be the one standing in the way of you getting to her."

"Don't you see, Annie? Losing you would be unbearable for me. Mac and Gabe will find Gabby. I'm not going to leave you here like a sitting duck by yourself with no protection at all. That would be foolish. And it would be the last thing in the world that Gabby would want. Remember how seriously she took her protective detail of you?"

"Yes, but..."

"No. Gabby would not want me to forsake you to help her. Yes, she's my sister and I love her. But she's also a trained private investigator. So are we on the same page?"

Annie looked up at him. "Yes," she said softly. "I just don't want anyone else to get hurt."

He reached out and cradled her face with his hands. "We'll get through this together."

She took another step forward and he wrapped his arms around her.

***

That night Annie sat in the living room with the TV on but not really paying attention to whatever show was on. She was becoming far too attached to Caleb. But as much as she kept telling herself that she wasn't capable of having a regular relationship with someone, she couldn't give up hope. What if there was even a one percent chance that her life could be different? That she could take a different path than her mom had?

And Caleb was the main reason for her having those feelings. After listening to what he had gone through in Afghanistan, she would be forever changed. The hurt and pain that he had experienced was something she would never be able to fully comprehend. But the fact that he had shared his journey made a huge difference to her. It made her think that maybe they weren't all that different after all. Maybe they both had their pain and past, but they could grow together.

But that would still mean that she would have to get over herself. Her doubts about whether she'd end up just like her mother.

Her fears about being codependent on a man. Maybe God was providing her a way to break through it all.

"Hey." Caleb walked into the room breaking her out of her thoughts.

"Any word on Gabby?"

"Nothing yet. But they plan to stay out all night if they have to. There's only so much ground to cover in Maxwell so they should be able to do it. I also just heard from Kane. He's trying to get the latest DEA intel on Vaughn's whereabouts."

She shivered just hearing his name. "You know, I want to be at a place where hearing his name doesn't bother me. But I'm not there yet."

He took her hand in his. "You can get there, though. I know you can."

"I've been thinking a lot about everything you told me about what happened to you in the war."

"You have?"

She nodded. "I'm so in awe of what you were able to do. Given all the pain and strife you went through. But listening to you talk about it all gives me some measure of hope."

He smiled. "I'm glad that you can take something from my sorrow. That's why I feel like we're more alike than you think. We've both had some painful experiences and we can relate to each other because of it."

"I look at you, at the burden you had to bear. It was certainly a heavier burden than mine. But here you are giving me the pep talk. I could use some of your strength."

"Like I said before, Annie, I couldn't have done it by myself. The Lord came through for me in a huge way." He squeezed her hand. "And don't discount how strong you are. Strength isn't just about the physical, it's about the emotional and the spiritual."

"I've never had anyone tell me that I was strong. I'm not used to hearing it."

"Don't ever underestimate yourself."

"Thanks for having faith in me."

Caleb's phone rang and he dropped her hand to pull it out of his phone. "It's Gabby!"

He put it on speaker and answered. "Gabby?"

"Caleb, thank God you answered."

"What's wrong? Where are you? We've been trying to contact you."

"I need you to come help me, please. I hurt my ankle and I can't walk. If you don't get here quickly, Silva's men will find me. Please come quickly."

"Mac and Gabe are in Maxwell trying to find you right now. What's the address? I'll send them and they'll be right there."

"No. I'm not in Maxwell. I'm in Atlanta."

"What?"

"It's a long story and I don't have time to explain. The address is 778 Murphy Street. Please hurry."

There were some voices in the background before the line went dead.

***

Annie looked at him. "We need to go now. Gabby's hurt and we're so much closer than Mac and Gabe."

He paused for a moment. He couldn't leave Annie alone. That was too risky. But he also didn't like the idea of taking her directly into the lion's den. But his baby sister needed him. She had begged him to help. Which made him think something was off, because come to think of it, he didn't think he had ever heard his sister beg for help in his entire life.

So he had to go save Gabby and get her out of there. But he also had to keep Annie safe. He looked over at Annie. And once again this woman amazed him. She was willing to put her own life in danger to try to save Gabby.

"You're right. Let's go." He grabbed his bag of supplies that Kane had gotten him and double-checked his sidearm. He wasn't quite sure how this was all going to go down but there was no time now to try to sketch out a fully developed plan. He'd just have to wing it as he went.

They got into the SUV they were currently driving that Gabe had provided him. He put the street address in the GPS and hit the gas.

"We can do this," Annie said. "Gabby's going to be all right. Like you said, she's one tough person."

Once again Annie was showing no fear. "You're becoming too good at this, you know that?"

"Just taking it all one step at a time." She paused. "What's our plan when we get there?"

That was the million dollar question. "A lot will depend on what is actually at this address."

"Why do you think she ended up somewhere in Atlanta investigating instead of Maxwell?"

"Maybe she got a different lead. Gabby is relentless. If she found new information that she thought would bring her closer to getting rock solid evidence against Silva, then she would act on it. She's not going to back down from a challenge."

"Even it if were dangerous."

"Yes. Even if." And that's what he feared the most—that Gabby had stepped right into the danger zone. And now his baby sister was hurt and calling him for help. He could only pray that they got there fast enough as he accelerated even further.

Annie pointed to the GPS. "Looks like we're just a couple minutes out. We're headed into an industrial district of town."

"Yeah. I'm going to park a little bit away because I have no idea what the situation will be at the actual address."

"Okay. That sounds like a good idea."

She might be saying that now, but he had a feeling she wasn't going to like the other part of his plan that he was currently developing on the fly. When he saw that he was a few blocks away, he stopped the car in front of a carpet company.

He reached into the back and grabbed his bag. Then he pulled a gun out of the bag. "Annie, I need you to listen to me closely."

"All right. I'm listening."

His eyes locked onto hers. "I'm going to need you to stay here in the car while I go inside."

She shook her head. "No way. I'm going in with you. It'll be better if there are two of us. I can help you. I promise."

"No. It's far too dangerous. I don't know what I'm going to be facing. And since Gabby is hurt, I'll have to probably carry her out of there, and I won't be able to protect you both at the same time."

She bit her bottom lip but didn't say anything.

"I need you to get in the driver's seat when I get out. If you feel threatened in any way, by anyone, no matter who they are, I want you drive away."

"All right."

"Can you promise me that you can do that?"

"Yes. I understand."

"And one more thing. I know you're not big on guns, but I'm leaving this Glock here with you." He placed the gun in the center console. "I turned the safety off. So all you need to do is point and shoot. You've done it before. You can do it again. But only if you have to. It's just an extra level of precaution. The first option is just to drive away. You got it?"

"Yes. I'll wait here and if there's anything suspicious. I'll drive away. I can loop back around if need be and pick you up."

"I'll be as fast as I can. I've texted Mac and Gabe, but their ETA is forty five minutes."

"Just go. Don't waste any more time with me. I promise I'll be fine here. Go get Gabby. She needs you now."

Without thinking, he leaned in and pressed his lips to hers. "I'll be back as soon as I can."

***

Caleb jogged the few blocks up to the address that Gabby had told him. When he reached the destination, he looked up to see a large two story building under construction. Gabby was somewhere in there and he intended to find her.

But he needed to be as quiet as possible in his search. Which was a little difficult given all the random debris scattered throughout on the ground. He'd clear the building room by room until he located where she was hiding.

He had to get in and find out what was going on. He entered one of the doors on the side that was open. The building wasn't fully constructed yet. It appeared that full lighting panels hadn't been installed throughout the building as it was still a work in progress. But a lamp in the corner provided a little light in the room. Other large pockets were completely dark. He didn't see any signs of activity. Could it be that Silva's men had already checked the building and left? Or worse, what if he was too late and they'd taken Gabby.

He had to be careful of his footing because he wasn't a hundred percent sure that all the flooring was solid. The last thing he needed to do was fall through the building and break a leg. There was too much riding on this.

Quickly he took the staircase by the door he entered to check out the second floor. He didn't hear a sound as he made his way room to room. "Gabby," he whispered. No response. And if Silva's men were present they were hiding and silent which didn't seem right to him. In fact, everything about this situation felt wrong.

It seemed like he was the only living thing in the building. But there was no way he was leaving that building without checking every single room.

By the time he'd cleared all the upstairs rooms, his pulse was racing. Because his gut was telling him that something was terribly wrong.

* * *

Annie sat on high alert in the SUV. She kept her hands on the wheel and her eyes peeled. But for the past few minutes, there had been nothing. No activity whatsoever. It was like a dead zone. And at this time of night, there wasn't anyone around. It was so quiet in the car she could hear her own breathing—which only added to her anxiety.

She debated taking the gun out of the console just in case she needed to access it quickly. But then she realized that the last thing in the world she wanted to do was to shoot another human being ever again. While she had no doubt she did the right thing in self defense when she shot Damon, it still weighed heavily on her. Because she had permanently injured another human. And that in and of itself hurt her heart.

She let out a breath and slightly lessened her grip on the wheel. It didn't appear that there were any threats out there in the night. She sat as patiently as she could watching the minutes tick by. Two, then five, then ten. Still no sign of anyone else or of Caleb. Her mind started rushing to worst case scenarios. What if Gabby was seriously injured?

When she looked at the clock again, she saw that it had only been fifteen minutes since Caleb had left. She needed to be more patient. These things take time and he would've been very cautious, especially because of Gabby's injuries.

Some movement on her left side caught her eye. She turned and looked out the car window down the street. Two men were walking in her direction, but on the opposite side of the street. Just as they were about to walk under one of the street lamps, she gasped. No, it couldn't be. But with each step she became more certain.

As one of the two faces came into clear view, she recognized it as a face she'd never forget. Damon Vaughn was right there. It had to be him. He was walking with a severe limp. And he was with another man. She squinted as they kept walking past where she was parked and in the direction of the building where Gabby was supposed to be at.

Was the other man Tim Silva? She'd seen a picture of him and it could've been him. Regardless, this wasn't good. The two of them were headed to where Caleb was, and he had no idea they were coming.

What should she do? She knew she wasn't a trained law enforcement officer. All of this was so out of her element. But she did have a gun. And right now, she couldn't leave Caleb and Gabby there like sitting ducks for Damon and Silva to take them out.

Lord, please protect Caleb and Gabby. I'll do all I can to help. Be with me as I try.

She took the gun, opened up the door and headed out into the night.

CHAPTER TWELVE

Caleb was over half way done clearing the building and no sign of anyone. His phone buzzed and he looked down to see a text message from Mac.

Get out of there now. It's a trap! Gabby's not there. Abort!

Immediately he feared that the building might blow. He didn't waste any time as he made his way back through the maze of construction equipment on the first floor, toward the side exit.

But that's when he heard deep male voices approaching. There's no way he could get out that door now. He'd backtrack and hunker down.

He strained to listen to the voices as they got closer.

"He has to be here somewhere," one man said quietly. "Ramsey ensured me that he'd come here looking for her. He's come through for us so far over the past two years. We have no reason to doubt him now."

What in the world? Then it hit him. Mike Ramsey—his own deputy police chief was the law enforcement mole. It wasn't FBI. It was Mike this whole time.

And by going to Mike, he had unwittingly put Gabby in harm's way. Where was she now? Did Mike hurt her? Anger surged through Caleb, but quickly he had to summon up all of his battlefield discipline and focus on the current threat.

"He's here somewhere. He wouldn't leave baby sister behind," the other man said. "Ramsey made sure that Gabby made the call to her brother to ensure that he would come riding in on his white horse to the rescue. We may have beaten him here. Let's check things out first to be on the safe side. If it's all clear, then we'll just wait for him to arrive and take him out."

He pulled his phone out and shot a quick text to Mac. Because Mac needed to know about the two men that were in this building now searching for him. At least he had the element of surprise. They didn't know that he knew they were there.

"Once we're done with him, then we can take care of Annie once and for all," one of them said.

No matter what, he couldn't allow that to happen. He wasn't concerned for his own safety or for that matter his own life. But he couldn't allow Annie to be harmed. He was so glad that she was in the safety of the car. He had his gun ready. He'd make a move when he needed to. But first he had to see how they were going to play it.

"You check downstairs and I'll check upstairs," the one guy said. "I'm glad we decided to take care of this personally instead of sending any of our guys. We can't afford any screw-ups this time. We need to deal with this problem once and for all. Then we can get on with our expansion plans. No more pesky roadblocks."

Ah, Caleb thought. Could it be that the two men in the building right now weren't Silva's hired thugs but were actually Silva and Vaughn? This was the perfect opportunity to arrest them both. He knew Mac was still about fifteen minutes out. Could he hold his ground until backup arrived? That was the best plan. He had to evade these guys but still keep them there so they could be arrested and tried for their crimes. The last thing he needed was a two against one shoot out.

He heard the footsteps above his head as one of the two men was going through the upstairs. He crouched down behind a stack of two by fours in a large closet on the ground floor.

"Well isn't this a surprise," the man on the first floor of the building said.

What was he talking about? Caleb leaned in and focused on what was being said.

"I'm not afraid of you, Damon."

Caleb felt like he was kicked in the gut at the sound of Annie's voice. Why in the world had she come into the building? This changed everything. He couldn't hide anymore. He had to go save Annie from this madman. He wouldn't let him attack her for a second time in her life.

***

Annie was putting on a brave face, but inside she was scared to death as she faced down Damon Vaughn. The man whose violent attack had changed her entire life. One lamp in the corner of the room provided enough light to see exactly who she was facing. Dark brown evil eyes that she would never forget. This was the man who had changed everything for her.

Damon took a step and grimaced. An all too familiar reminder of what she did to him.

"Where's your cop friend? He can't be too far away. I can't imagine that he'd leave you alone with the wolves on the prowl." He gave her a sinister grin that rocked her to the core.

"I don't know where he is," she answered. Although she prayed he would come soon. She had the gun in her right hand, protected by the dark shadows so that he couldn't see it. She could try to shoot him right now. But he hadn't done anything yet. And what if she missed? In her head, she started to play out the various scenarios. What was the best course of action? *Lord, please help me.*

"The cop doesn't even matter at this moment. This is even better than I could've imagined."

"What do you mean?" The longer she kept him talking, the better, because she knew that Caleb couldn't be too far away, could he? What if she'd missed him on the way to the building? What if he had taken a different route? Unlikely. She had to just stay focused on staying alive.

"What's going on down here?" Silva walked down the stairs and into the dimly lit room.

"You're just in time," Damon said. "I'm sorry, Tim."

"Sorry for what?" Silva asked him as he walked closer.

Damon raised his gun in the air, and pulled the trigger. A loud gunshot pierced through the night as the bullet struck Silva in the head.

She stood stunned as Tim Silva dropped to the ground. Damon had just killed his cousin. But why? She had no idea what he was doing next, but he had just shown that he was capable of murder.

Then Damon turned to her. "You're next but a clean gunshot to the head is way too nice of a death for you, little Annie."

A surge of fear shot through her as she remembered how he used to call her that name a decade ago. "What are you going to do to me?"

"Make you pay for what you did to me. Did you think I would forget? I have to live like this every single day because of you." He motioned toward his right leg. "Imagine how surprised and happy I was when I found out that the thorn in Silva's side was a woman named Annie Thomas from Florida. It didn't take much investigating at all to find out that it was you."

"I had no idea he was your cousin."

"You have no idea how long I've thought about seeing you again. With every step I take, every painful step, I think of the day that I will get my revenge. And it looks like that day is today."

"Why did you kill Silva?"

"Because it was time for me to be in charge. He had his time. He was being unreasonable about the future plans and it was becoming too cumbersome to deal with him. He was more of a liability than an asset. Just like you. And this now with you here, it provides me with the perfect way to get rid of him. The murder will be pinned on you. But you'll also be dead so you don't have to worry about that."

He took a step toward her and she lifted her gun, which had been obscured by the dark spot she was standing in the room.

"Hey now," he said. "You're not going to shoot me again, little Annie."

"I'd prefer not to, but you're not giving me much of a choice."

He sputtered out some foul insults at her. Then he lunged toward her. She hesitated, not wanting to pull the trigger. Not again.

But a gunshot rang out loudly. It wasn't from her gun, though. Damon staggered a few steps and then stumbled to the ground holding onto his right shoulder.

Caleb walked further into the room with his gun still drawn. "Annie, are you all right?"

"Yes." She tried to understand what had just happened. She didn't have the will to pull the trigger again, but she hadn't needed to because Caleb had been there.

He went over to Damon and pulled out his handcuffs. Then he started reading Damon his rights.

"Is he going to make it?" she couldn't help but ask.

"Yes. I shot him in the shoulder. Should be clean through and through."

Damon lay down on the ground moaning in pain. But immobilized by the handcuffs and no longer any threat to her.

Caleb strode over to her. "I'm so sorry. I didn't act any faster because I needed a clear shot."

She let out a breath and then flung her arms around him. "I was so afraid."

"You faced him down like a battle hardened warrior. But why in the world were you even in here?"

"I saw them walking down the street. I knew it was two of them and I wasn't sure what was going on inside with you and Gabby. So I felt I had to come and warn you."

"That was so brave of you, Annie. I wish you hadn't risked your life for mine, but I appreciate your courage."

"I had to risk my life because you would've done the same thing for me." She took in a deep breath as she tried to steady herself. "But what about Gabby?"

"She's not here. I got a text from Mac saying it was a trap. So I don't know what happened to her. Mac should be here any minute." He paused. "And I found out my deputy Mike Ramsey is the mole. We'll have to track him down."

"I'm so sorry."

She heard voices from the outside. Mac and Gabe rushed into the building with their guns drawn.

"It's okay," Caleb said.

Annie stood for a moment by herself as Caleb recounted the events of the night. Gabe took Damon out of the building for medical attention and to place him into FBI custody. They were calling backup to retrieve Silva's body.

Caleb came back over to her.

"Any word on Gabby?"

"Yes. Mike took her. He was the one that made her make that phone call. But Gabby being Gabby was able to finally convince him that he shouldn't be working on the dark side. He turned himself in and let Gabby go. She pulled off an amazing feat."

"Wow. I'm so glad that she's okay."

He wrapped his arms around her tightly. "When I heard your voice tonight, and I knew you were walking into the line of fire, I realized that I didn't know how I'd ever be able to keep living my life if you weren't in it."

"What?" she asked, as she felt the tears start to flow.

"I know that you worry that we're incompatible, that we come from two different worlds. But Annie, if that's true, then I want to leave my world and step into yours."

"Caleb, no. You don't have to leave your world. I don't want you to change. You're a special man. I've never met anyone as noble, caring, and strong as you are. And even though I tried to convince myself otherwise, I can't imagine ever being with anyone else."

"I've fallen in love with you, Annie Thomas."

Her heart felt like it was going to explode hearing those words. But even more than the words, she could feel the love that he had for her. "I love you, too. I thank God that he brought you to me. That you have shown me that no matter what we've been through, we can push through it."

"Together we can."

***

Caleb took in a deep breath of the Georgia spring air mixed with the smell of the steaks sizzling on the grill. It had only been a week since Vaughn's arrest, but so much had happened.

And now in his backyard surrounded by his friends and family, it was time to start over in so many ways.

Mac, Gabe, and Kane were all hanging out around the grill with him. Many of his officers were there and some FBI agents that Mac knew. But it still ate at him that his deputy, Mike Ramsey, a man with a lifetime on the force, had betrayed him. Mike had taken Silva's money and done the dirty work in return. He finally understood exactly how Annie could have trust issues with law enforcement. Because he now felt the sting of betrayal in a very personal way.

"So has the FBI been cleared of the possibility of a mole?" Kane asked the group.

"Yes," Gabe said. "Every indication we have is that Mike acted alone, and he put out misinformation about the FBI having a mole to throw people off the trail. We were so focused on the FBI angle, we didn't even think it could be someone that close to us. Mike used his relationship with Mac and Caleb to get information. He also passed on the information about the DEA safe house to Silva."

"It's sickening," Mac said. "And last I heard, he's trying to craft a plea deal. That dirty cop kidnapped our sister. I think he should rot."

"What could he trade? Silva is dead and Vaughn is behind bars waiting for trial," Gabe said.

"He still has intel," Caleb said. "Information about the rest of the Silva organization, the remaining higher ups. I understand why a plea could be on the table. And even as much as what he did hurts, we will just have to accept a deal if one is struck. But regardless, he'll see prison time. It's just a question of how much."

"Not enough in my book, brother," Mac said.

"Well, word on the street is that the Silva organization is in complete disarray right now," Kane said. "With the two top ranking guys out of the picture, either someone will rise up and take over or they'll all become free agents and latch themselves onto the next big thing. Or one of Silva's competitors."

"Today isn't the day to rehash all of this." Mac looked at Caleb. "Let's be thankful for what we have and enjoy this day."

Mac was saying exactly what Caleb was thinking. Then Caleb noticed that Mac's eyes diverted over to the backyard gate. And that was because Jen Spencer and her little girl Cindy had just arrived. Jen was carrying a cake plate. Mac had been in love with Jen since high school. "Mac, why don't you go help Jen. She's got her hands full."

"Yeah, of course." Mac walked off to go help Jen.

Caleb hoped that one day his brother could find happiness like what he had found. As he looked over at Annie with her long hair blowing in the wind with Buddy right beside her with his Frisbee, he thanked God for sending such an amazing woman into his life.

***

Annie took in the festive atmosphere as the barbeque was in full force in Caleb's backyard. Caleb had insisted on having everyone over. There had been so much darkness and fear, it felt amazing to sit in the sun with a big glass of lemonade and hear the laughter from the people surrounding her—friends and family. Things she didn't really have before. And now it all seemed like it could be possible.

Caleb looked over from the grill and gave her a big smile. He loved her. That much she knew, and she loved him back. It was unlike anything she'd ever experienced in her life.

She glanced over and saw Hope approaching with Sasha close by her side. For a moment her pulse kicked up, but then she had to remind herself that this nightmare was over.

Hope grabbed her in a big hug. "How're you doing?"

"Much better. I'm sleeping through the night for the first time in a long time."

Sasha smiled at her. "I wanted to apologize again for causing you any distress. That was never my intent. I am so sorry for everything you've gone through."

"I appreciate your apology, but Hope helped me understand that you were just trying to do your job."

"And that's what I plan to do. I plan to prosecute Damon Vaughn to the fullest extent of the law. He will never be able to hurt you again. I feel like justice will get served. And to me that's very important."

Gabby walked over to them. "Can I join you ladies? I feel like we're kind of outnumbered by the guys here."

Caleb had invited all of his officers except Mike. Who, according to Caleb, was currently in jail.

"Who is that handsome dark haired mysterious man talking to Gabe?" Sasha asked.

"That's Kane. He's with the DEA," Annie said. And she could tell by the look on Sasha's face that Sasha might have taken an interest in Kane.

"I could introduce you," Hope offered.

"Sure. Maybe later," Sasha said.

"Annie, can you help me out with something in the kitchen for just a quick minute?" Gabby asked.

"Sure." She followed Gabby inside the house.

"I actually just wanted to get you alone for a minute," Gabby said.

"What's going on?"

"I know I was kinda hard on you when we first met. I'm pretty protective of my brothers. As you know, we lost our parents, and we're a tight knit unit."

Annie smiled. "Believe me, I know that."

"But I wanted you to know that I want you here. I've never seen my brother this happy. When he's around you, there's real joy in his eyes."

Hearing Gabby's heartfelt words touched her.

"I have to tell you, Annie, when he came back from Afghanistan from his final deployment, we thought for a while that we might not ever get our brother back. I know he dealt with many things during the war. And he bounced back eventually.

But now he seems like the fog of war has finally lifted off of him. And I think I have you to thank for that."

"Well, it works both ways, because he helped me get over the fears of my past. So we are growing stronger together."

"I'm not much of a hugger," Gabby said. "But for this, I'll make an exception." Gabby reached out and gave her a tight hug.

"Thanks, Gabby. It means a lot."

Caleb walked into the kitchen and his eyes widened. "Uh oh. What's going on in here?"

"Nothing. Just a minute of girl talk," Gabby said as she looked at Annie.

"Good. Cause I'm about to serve up the food. So come back out and grab a plate."

"I'll go and see if Mac needs any help." Gabby walked out of the kitchen leaving them alone.

"Seriously, was she giving you a hard time?" Caleb asked her.

"No. Just the opposite, actually."

"Great, because I can't have my little sister giving my girlfriend grief." He leaned down and kissed her. "Now let's go celebrate. We have so much to be thankful for."

EPILOGUE

Ten months later

"**B**uddy, sit." Annie held up the treat and the black lab sat dutifully. She'd been spending a lot of time with Buddy and had come a long way with his training. But more than anything else, she just enjoyed his love and company. Even more than that, she enjoyed the love and company of his owner.

"So you ready to take them on a walk?" Caleb asked as he walked into the room.

"Definitely." She'd settled down very easily in Maxwell. She had a small apartment and had been working full time at Pa's Diner. It was nothing that she thought she'd ever wanted, but turned out to be everything she needed.

Caleb leashed up Buddy and Bailey and handed her Buddy's leash. "So I saw Mitzi when I was in town. She mentioned that your lease would be expiring in three months."

"Yes. But I already talked to her, and she said I could renew it if I wanted. I really like it there, so I think it makes the most sense to stay put. I hate moving, and it's big enough for me." They headed down the sidewalk walking side by side with the dogs. She didn't think things could get any better than they were.

"About that. I don't want you to renew the lease."

"Why in the world not? You thought that apartment was the perfect fit for me."

He shook his head. "I did think it was perfect. But it's not anymore."

"Why not?"

He stopped and turned toward her. "Because of this." He dropped down on one knee, and when he did, both dogs sat down beside him.

Her pulse thumped wildly as she realized what he was doing.

He reached into his pocket and pulled out a simple, but elegant square cut diamond. "Annie Thomas, you're everything that I never thought I could possibly find in one person. You're strong, beautiful, smart and talented. But most of all, I love your caring and devoted heart. I want to spend the rest of my life with you, if you will have me. Annie, will you marry me?"

As he said the words, Buddy lifted his big furry black paw up in the air and that did it. Tears of joy fell down her cheeks. "Yes. Absolutely, yes."

He stood up and slid the ring on her finger and the dogs barked in approval.

"I love you so much, Caleb."

"I love you, too."

He kissed her with the promise of the rest of their lifetimes together. No longer weighed down by the past, she opened up her heart fully to the man she loved.

DANGER IN THE DEEP SOUTH SERIES

Book 1: Lethal Action (Hope & Gabe)
Book 2: Devoted Defender (Annie & Caleb)
Book 3: (Jen & Mac)

Excerpt from Lethal Action: Danger
in the Deep South Book 1

Five years. Hope Finch was celebrating her fifth year anniversary as an attorney at the prestigious New York law firm of Rice and Taylor by chugging down another cup of lukewarm coffee. She'd lost count at mug number six. As a fifth year associate, she still had a lot to prove. Not only to the firm, but to herself as well.

She glanced at the clock on her computer screen and saw that she'd worked late into the night and skipped dinner again. Nothing unusual for her. The Wakefield trial was taking up all of her time—and then some. But there was no way she was going to say she couldn't handle the workload. As a midlevel associate, she should be able to run with the big boys. Or at least pretend like she could. If that meant coffee would be her only source of sustenance then so be it. If she wanted to make partner within three years, then she had to stick to the game plan.

Hope shutdown her computer and grabbed her laptop bag embroidered with the bright red R&T logo. It was very possible she'd still put in a little bit more time working tonight at home. Also part of her normal routine.

The big New York City law firm was relatively quiet for a weeknight. Only a couple of other associates were working away in their offices. She felt a tiny shred of guilt for leaving, but then quickly dismissed it. She was still on track for getting all of her work done in time for trial and sleep was necessary. She couldn't afford to make any mistakes right now. There was too much on the line. Both for her client and for her.

When the cold winter New York air blew against her face, she was glad to be headed home to her cozy apartment. It cost her a good chunk of her lawyer salary, but it was worth it. She paid a hefty price to be close to her office, and she still lived in a five hundred foot box.

Cinching her pink pea coat tightly around her waist, she walked quickly down the dark street. Even at this hour, there were still plenty of people walking around. She loved the anonymity and hustle and bustle of the city. It gave her the freedom she felt like she'd earned. She never understood how people could live in small towns where everyone knew every detail about your life. If she had it her way, no one would know anything about her. Except what she chose to share with them.

When she arrived at her high-rise apartment door, she turned the key in the lock, and dropped her bag on the floor. Immediately, she kicked off her tall heels and unbuttoned her grey suit jacket. Home sweet home. It wasn't much, but it was hers, and for that she was proud.

She started to reach for the light switch but a strong hand grabbed her wrist throwing her off balance. She screamed as her pulse thumped wildly. The hand moved to her mouth and the other wrapped securely around her waist pulling her into him. The intruder stood behind her, and she couldn't see him.

This was it. This man was going to kill her. He was strong. She was no match for him. In that moment, she found herself clicking back through the events of her life like a movie reel. Her horrible childhood front and center. Not enough time to make all of her dreams come true and to fully recover from her past. Wondering how much time she still had left. And filled with regret. She fought harder.

"Stop struggling. I'm not here to hurt you," he said. "I'm Special Agent Gabe Marino. I'm a federal agent. I work for the FBI."

The FBI? What was an FBI agent doing in her apartment? She didn't believe him, so she kept fighting. She bit down hard on his hand, and he let out a groan. Unfortunately, he didn't let go. Not willing to give up, she gathered up her strength and stomped on his foot.

Nothing was working though.

"Listen to me, Ms. Finch. I am going to drop my arms and step away from you. Don't scream." He slowly pulled his hand away from her mouth and loosened his grip. Then he turned on the lights, and she got her first look at her assailant. He was tall with short dark hair and chocolate colored eyes. He wore a dark suit and a striped navy tie. He looked the part of an FBI agent, but he could be anyone.

"Here, let me show you." He slowly reached into his suit jacket and pulled out his credentials. He showed her his FBI badge and identification.

His identification looked legitimate, but she also knew it was easy to forge credentials if you had the right resources. She didn't believe him yet. "Why would an FBI agent resort to breaking and entering?" she asked.

"I didn't break into your apartment. Actually, I have a warrant." He reached into his pocket and handed it to her. "Go ahead, take a look."

She didn't want to take her eyes off of him, but she glanced down quickly and read the warrant. This guy might actually be legitimate. The fact that he hadn't hurt her yet added to his credibility. But what if he was trying to gain her trust only to hurt her? Hadn't she had enough struggles in her life?

"What do you want with me?"

He stood with his hands in his pockets. "Information. I need to know what your involvement is with Carlos Nola."

She took a step back providing her a little distance. "Mr. Nola is a board member of Wakefield Corporation. My biggest client at Rice and Taylor. Or I guess I should say that Wakefield Corporation is technically a client of my firm. Not me specifically. I work on their cases. Have since I started working there."

"I know that."

"If you know so much about me, then why did you have to break into my apartment? Why not set up a meeting with me at the firm?"

"Because I needed to be discreet. I'm working on a very sensitive case."

"I don't understand what you're after here." She looked up into his dark eyes and wondered what was really going on. If he was really FBI and asking questions about her client, that couldn't be good. He definitely had her attention.

"We can do this the easy way or the hard way, Ms. Finch."

She crossed her arms not appreciative of his bossy tone. "I'm not saying another word, Mr. Marino, until you explain why you're really here. If you really are a federal agent then you know that I can't reveal privileged information about my firm's client, Wakefield Corporation."

"It's not Wakefield I'm that interested in. At least not directly. It's Carlos Nola. Like I said, I have a reasonable suspicion that you're involved with him and his questionable business practices. You'll get much more leniency if you work with us rather than if you try to protect him. So let me help you."

Could this really be happening? What was Nola involved in that was getting this scrutiny from the FBI? "Mr. Nola lives in Georgia. I've worked with him, and met him about five or so times in person, and every single time he was entirely professional. I would like to help you, but I really have no idea what you're talking about. He's a legitimate businessman. Respected in his community."

"This is about what is going on in his community—Maxwell, Georgia. That's where Wakefield's home office is."

"I'm well aware of that," she shot back. She wasn't telling this suit anything. She wasn't guilty, so that led her to believe that he was purely on a fishing expedition. She'd worked enough government investigations of big corporations to sense when there was actual evidence. If he had solid evidence he certainly wouldn't be hounding her.

"And you're sure there's nothing you want to tell me?" He took a step toward her.

"How do I even know you're from the FBI? For all I know you work for Cyber Future."

"Ah." He smiled. "No, I'm definitely a federal agent. How is the litigation between Wakefield and Cyber Future going?"

"That is not your concern, Mr. Marino. Now I'm going to have to ask you to leave my apartment."

"Are you sure you want to do that?"

"Yes. Please leave."

He cocked his head to the side. "If you are innocent, it's in your best interest not to say we had this conversation with anyone at your law firm. And if you're working with Nola, you're in danger. So don't say that you haven't been officially warned. This conversation isn't over, though. We'll be speaking again soon."

Before she could say anything he turned and walked out of her door.

"No, we won't," she said to out loud to herself.

What should she do? Should she tell the partners at the firm? No. First, she needed to figure out what was really going on. And that's exactly what she planned to do. If she went to her supervising partner at the firm right now he might pull her off the case. So she'd have to get to the bottom of this on her own. A constant theme of her life.

The litigation between Wakefield and Cyber Future had gotten ugly. The breach of contract case should have been all business and routine, but it had gotten personal between both the executives and the lawyers representing the two companies. Cyber Future wanted to take down her client. Cyber Future was quickly becoming a competitor of Wakefield. Was Cyber Future behind this FBI inquiry? She certainly wouldn't put it past them. Cyber Future was out for blood.

***

Gabe Marino wrapped his navy scarf tightly around his neck and let out a deep breath. Hope Finch knew that he didn't have a solid case against her. Even getting the warrant was difficult. She put on a good show that was for sure. When she looked at him with her big brown eyes and played dumb, he almost believed her. She would have most people fully believing her innocence, but she'd been working with Nola for five years. She admitted that much herself.

He'd been watching her for the past few days. All she did was go back and forth from the office keeping very long hours. It didn't even appear that she even took a lunch break. He pictured her eating some microwavable meal at her desk and drinking coffee made in a fancy espresso machine purchased by the law firm.

He hadn't really known what to expect. Her file had made clear that she was a rising star at Rice and Taylor. She'd graduated top of her law school class. Obviously smart. She was also an attractive woman. Not that he was taking particular note of that. Every time he'd seen her over the past few days she'd worn her long blonde hair pulled back in a low ponytail. Her suits looked expensive. Maybe even designer. But he wasn't surprised given that she worked at one of the most prestigious law firms in the city and had the stellar salary to match. She would need to look the part. Her salary made his look laughable. It irked him that big firm lawyers were so grossly overpaid as they defended massive corporations. Meanwhile, federal agents who often put their lives on the line were often barely making ends meet.

He had a job to do, and he couldn't help the feeling that Hope was right in the middle of it all. He didn't believe in coincidences. Too many unanswered questions made him uneasy. Was she part of the plot that Nola was cooking up, or was she in potential danger? Gabe believed that Nola was running several illegal businesses in Maxwell using Wakefield resources to help him. Those businesses included drug trafficking and money laundering. All things that had no place in Maxwell.

As he walked to his hotel, he tried to focus. The cold New York City weather was messing with his brain. He could never live up there, and he couldn't get back to Georgia soon enough.

This case was personal for him. He worked in the Atlanta field office of the FBI, but he was born and raised in Maxwell, Georgia. And he planned to always live there. The commute to Atlanta was forty five minutes. But it was well worth the drive and extra gas to live in Maxwell and maintain his quiet lifestyle. A lifestyle that was threatened by people like Carlos Nola.

There was something sinister going on in his town—the town he loved. And he intended to stop it. Hope Finch might be the key to unraveling the entire mystery. She knew more than she was letting on. She had to.

Carlos Nola was up to no good. Gabe knew that Nola was using Wakefield Corporation to help further his criminal enterprise that was infecting Maxwell. What he didn't know is if it was only Nola who was involved. How far did Nola's influence reach?

Hope had been telling the truth about her meetings with Nola. His research indicated that they'd met recently in New York and periodically at her firm before that. Even if she wasn't working for him as part of his criminal ventures, she could still be useful in his investigation. As one of the Wakefield lawyers, she'd have unprecedented access to Nola. He wasn't giving up on her. There was still a lot of work to do. And Hope Finch was the center of it all.

***

Hope didn't know what to think when she'd gotten the email from her boss, Sam Upton, telling her that they needed to meet first thing in the morning. Sam was the partner in charge of the litigation between Wakefield and Cyber Future. Hope worried that she'd done something wrong. She recounted the work she'd completed over the past week. Nothing stood out in her mind that she could've messed up, but Sam was such an important partner at the firm she couldn't afford to make any mistakes. Not even a small one. If he removed her from the case, she'd be devastated.

She took a deep breath and smoothed down her suit jacket before walking to his office. His door was open, but she still knocked. Sam was nice enough to work for, but there was still a gulf between him being a partner and her being a mid-level associate. A pretty gigantic gulf—he held all the power, and she held none.

"Come in, Hope," he said. Sam wore a custom made navy suit and blue striped tie. He'd been working at the firm for decades, and his personal tailor often visited him at the office.

She started trying to figure out how to explain away whatever it was that she must have messed up.

"So," he said, "I've actually got some exciting news. Or at least I hope you'll think so because I do."

"Okay," she replied. Now he really had her attention.

"First, let me say that you've been doing great work on the Wakefield case. Really performing above your level and everyone has noticed including the client. They've been highly impressed with your dedication to this case. You've really been keeping this train on the tracks."

"Thank you, sir." She clasped her hands with nervous excitement.

"How many times have I told you not to sir me, Hope?"

"I'm sorry."

He smiled. "And stop apologizing. Just listen up for a minute. You know I was supposed to try this case with Harry. But there's been an emergency international arbitration for one of our biggest clients. Harry's on a plane to Brussels right now and won't be back for a couple of months. I decided to send him because they needed a partner over there right now with his international experience."

She started to try to process what all of this would mean. If Harry wasn't going to try the case with Sam, then who was?

He leaned forward in his chair. "Since you know the case so well, I want you to go to Maxwell, Georgia, and get us set up for trial next week. And then at trial you'll be second chair. My number two. Also means a literal seat at counsel's table and you examining and crossing select witnesses."

"Second chair?" She heard herself say the words out loud but couldn't fathom it.

"Yes, you've earned it. I know associates don't get much trial experience around here since our cases have such a high dollar value. So you need to take this one head on. You'll be working with our local counsel in Maxwell to prepare for trial. I'll be coming down there in a few days, but I want you on the ground now. You up for this?"

She didn't even know how to respond. "Of course I am." This is exactly what she wanted. What she'd been working so hard for five years at the firm to show that she had what it takes to make it in big law. This was her time to shine.

"Great. Now have your secretary book you a flight for this afternoon. Get out of here and pack. I want you on a plane and in Maxwell by this evening."

She nodded realizing it was probably better not to start gushing to her boss. "Thank you, I won't let you down."

She remained calm until she got back to her office and shut the door. Then she let out a squeal as she hopped around her small office. Second chair! And getting to go to Maxwell ahead of Sam to work with the client and the local law firm. This was a once in a career opportunity for someone like her. She hadn't felt this happy in years. If ever.

She couldn't let this chance slip away. She'd have to be on the top of her game the entire time. While Sam cared about all of his clients, he'd been college roommates with Lee Wakefield, the CEO of Wakefield Corporation. So Sam took this case personally. He wouldn't accept anything but her best—and then some. She'd proven herself to be a hard worker, and it was nice to see that it was actually paying off. But her work was far from done.

Hope gave her secretary instructions on booking the flight to leave New York around lunchtime and then went home to pack. She'd never been to Georgia. Much less the small town of Maxwell. This would be an experience she'd never forget. And there was also an added bonus. Now she could ensure she wouldn't run into agent whatever his name was again. Their altercation last night was strange, and it bothered her that he was making allegations against Carlos Nola.

A tiny shred of doubt crept into her thoughts. What if the FBI agent was right and Nola was involved in some illegal activity? Could her work actually be protecting and aiding a criminal? No. She refused to believe that.

She'd had a few meetings with Nola in New York, and he always seemed entirely professional. Friendly, a gentleman, and with a shrewd business acumen. There had never been any hint of impropriety in any of their discussions. She'd spoken to him on the phone quite a bit lately because of trial preparation, and she'd experienced no red flags of any kind. Wakefield Corporation was also a very well thought of business with board members who were highly respected in the community. No, there simply had to be some mistake on the FBI's part.

The FBI was mistaken, and it was her job to protect her client, Wakefield Corporation. Nola wouldn't do anything to jeopardize the business, because as a board member, he had a vested interest to stay above board with all of his business dealings.

She wasn't one to just sit back, though. She planned to find out what the FBI was really after before it was too late.

***

Click to here to buy LETHAL ACTION.

WINDY RIDGE LEGAL THRILLER SERIES

Book 1: Trial & Tribulations (A 2016 Selah Awards Finalist)
Book 2: Fatal Accusation

Excerpt from Trial & Tribulations: A
Windy Ridge Legal Thriller

When managing partner Chet Carter called, you answered—and you answered promptly. Just yesterday Olivia Murray had been summoned to Chet's corner office and told to pack her bags for a new case that would take her from Washington, DC to the Windy Ridge suburb of Chicago.

But this wasn't just any case. She would be defending a New Age tech company called Astral Tech in a lawsuit filed by its biggest competitor.

As she stepped out of her red Jeep rental, the summer breeze blew gently against her face. She stared up at the mid sized office building with a prominent sparkling blue moon on the outside, and she had to admit she was a bit intimidated. It wasn't the litigation aspect that bothered her, though. It was the subject matter.

She threw her laptop bag over her shoulder, adjusted her black suit jacket, and walked toward the door. Ready for anything. Or at least she hoped she was.

The strong smell of incense hit her as her first heeled foot stepped through the door. She thought it was a bit cliché for a New Age company to be burning incense in the reception area, but maybe it was to be expected. It reinforced her thoughts that this was all a money making operation—not a group of actual believers in this stuff.

The perky young blonde behind the minimalist glass desk looked up at her. "How can I help you?"

"Hi, I'm Olivia Murray from the law firm of Brown, Carter, and Reed."

The young woman's brown eyes widened. "Oh, yes, Ms. Murray. I'm Melanie." She stood and shook Olivia's hand. "Let me know if you need anything while you're here. The team is expecting you. I'll take you to the main conference room now."

"Thank you." Everything was already proceeding as normal. She couldn't let this whole New Age thing mess with her head. And besides that, she had her faith to get her through this.

Melanie led her down the hall to a conference room and knocked loudly before opening the large door. "Ms. Murray, please go on in."

Olivia didn't really know what she expected, but what she saw was a table full of suits arguing. She let out a breath. Regular litigation. Just like she had thought.

A man stood up from the table. "You must be our lawyer from BCR?" He wore an impeccably tailored navy suit with a red tie. He had short dark hair with a little gray at the temples and piercing green eyes.

"Yes, I'm Olivia Murray."

"Great. This is the Astral Tech leadership team. Don't let our yelling worry you. That's how we best communicate." He laughed. "I'm Clive Township, the CEO of Astral Tech, and this is my trusted inner circle."

A striking woman rose and offered her hand. "I'm Nina Marie Crane, our Chief Operating Officer."

"Wonderful to meet you," Olivia said.

Clive nodded toward a tall thin man with black hair who stood and shook her hand. "And this is our financial voice of reason, Matt Tinley."

"I serve as our Chief Financial Officer," Matt said.

Everyone greeted her warmly, but she felt an undercurrent of tension in the room. It was now her job as their attorney to get this litigation under control and that also meant getting them under control. Half the battle of litigation was controlling your own client before you could even begin to take on the adversary.

"Have a seat and we'll get you up to speed," Clive said.

She sat down in a comfortable dark blue chair at the oblong oak table and pulled out her laptop to take any relevant notes. She opened up her computer, but mainly she wanted to get the lay of the land.

"So the more I can learn about your company and the complaint that Optimism has filed against you the better. One of the first things I'll have to work on is the document collection and fact discovery effort. To be able to do that, I need the necessary background. I'll be happy to go over the discovery process with you, too, at some point so we're all on the same page."

"Where do you want to start?" Nina Marie asked.

"It would be helpful if you gave me a more detailed explanation of your company. I did my own research, but I'd love to hear it from you. Then we can move onto the legal claims brought against you by Optimism."

"Nina Marie is the driving force behind Astral Tech. So I'll let her explain our business," Clive said. "I'm more of the big picture guy and Matt is our number cruncher."

"Sounds good," Olivia said.

Nina Marie smiled. The thin auburn haired woman wore tortoiseshell glasses. Her hair was swept up into a loose bun, and she wore a black blazer with a rose colored blouse. "Astral Tech was my baby, but Clive has the financial backing and business acumen to make it happen."

"I'd like to hear all about it," Olivia said.

"We're a company specializing in bringing New Age theories and ideas into the tech space. We felt like we filled a void in that area. Yes, New Age has been quite popular for years now, but no company has really brought New Age into the current technology arena and made it work for the next generation. Through the Astral Tech app and other electronic means, we're making New Age relevant again. Our target audience is youth and young professionals. We don't even try to reach the baby boomers and beyond because it's a losing battle. They're too traditional, and they're not as tech savvy. We have to target our energy on the demographic that makes the most sense for our product."

"Excuse my ignorance, but you use New Age as a blanket term. I need a bit of education on what exactly you mean in the context of your business."

Nina Marie clasped her hands together in front of her. "Of course. I think a woman like you is in our key demographic. I would love to hear your thoughts on all of this. But to answer your question, New Age is a lot more than incense and meditation, although that is definitely a part of it. New Age is a way of life. A way of spiritually connecting. We care about the whole body—the environment, mysticism, spirituality. And we do that in an innovative way through the Astral Tech app that starts you on your path of self exploration from day one. You have to download it and try it for yourself. It will definitely help you understand our issues in the litigation better."

"Yes, the litigation. I read the complaint on the plane. Optimism's central claim is that Astral Tech actually stole the app from them."

Clive jumped in and leaned forward resting his arms on the table. "It's a totally bogus lawsuit. That's why we're hiring a firm like yours to nip this in the bud. We don't want any copycat litigation. This app was developed totally in house by Astral Tech employees. To say that there is any theft is absolutely false. We certainly didn't steal it. It's just a trumped up charge."

"What about the other claim regarding defamation?"

Clive nodded. "The defamation claim is actually a bit more concerning to me because it's subjective. We won't have a technical expert that can testify about that like we have on the actual theft claim."

She sat up in her seat. "What was said by Astral Tech that they are claiming is defamatory?"

"A few off handed comments about Optimism and their lack of integrity. They claim they're part of the New Age movement, but some of their actions indicate otherwise."

"Could you be more specific?"

"I can elaborate," Nina Marie said. "Optimism isn't really centered on New Age techniques in the same way we are. Their original founder, Earl Ward, was a connoisseur of many New Age techniques, but when he passed away Optimism's purpose shifted a bit under Layton Alito's rule, solidifying their allegiance to the dark arts. Layton is a ruthless leader who doesn't tolerate any type of dissent amongst his ranks."

Olivia felt her eyes widen, but she tried to hide her surprise. "Are you serious?"

"Yes, very," Nina Marie said.

"And Astral Tech isn't like that?" She couldn't help herself. She had to ask. It was better to know.

"We're a big tent. We don't want to alienate anyone who is seeking a spiritual journey," Clive said.

Well, that wasn't exactly a denial. What had she stepped into here? "And why New Age?"

Clive smiled. "Think about this as a lawyer. A businessperson. The world is becoming more and more open minded about spirituality. Which is obviously a good thing. Let everyone do what they want. We're moving away from strict codes of morality to something that fits with the modern person in this country. It's in. It's now. That's why we do it. We're using principles that have been popular for the past few decades and bringing them into the tech arena."

"For some of us, it's more than just about what makes money and make sense," Nina Marie said. "I'm proud to say that I'm a believer. A strong spiritual being. Those things have value. What we're doing matters. We have the ability to revolutionize the way people think about New Age principles."

Olivia could feel Nina Marie's dark eyes on her trying to evaluate whether she was truly friend or foe. A strange uneasiness settled over her. There was more to all of this than Nina Marie was saying. This was much larger than a lawsuit. Spiritual forces were at work here.

Focusing on the task at hand, she stared at her laptop and the page of notes she'd typed while hearing her clients talk. "I'll need to make sure you have a proper litigation hold in place to collect all relevant documents. I'll also want to talk to your IT person on staff right away about preserving all documents. The last thing we want to do is play cute and get sanctioned by the court. If Astral Tech has nothing to hide, then there's no reason to be evasive."

"But that's the thing," Matt said. "We believe we haven't broken any laws, but we also believe in our privacy and that of our customers."

Olivia nodded. "We should be able to petition the court for a protective order for any sensitive information that is turned over in the litigation, including customer lists. That's something we can handle."

Nina Marie stood up from her chair. "Let me take you to the office space we have set up for you while you're working here on this case."

"Thank you." While she was eager to get to work, she wasn't so excited about being alone with Nina Marie. But she followed the woman out of the conference room and down the hall, reminding herself that Nina Marie was still the client.

Nina Marie stopped abruptly about half way down the corridor. "I know this will sound a bit strange, but I'm getting a really interesting vibe from you."

"Vibe?"

"Yes. Do you have any interest in learning more about New Age spirituality? Anything like that?"

"No. That's not really my thing." She held back her direct answer which would've been totally unprofessional. She didn't feel comfortable in this environment, but she was also torn between her job and her faith. Could she really do both? Would defending a company like Astral Tech really be possible?

Conflicted feelings shot through her. No, she didn't believe in aliens or monsters, but she definitely believed in good and evil. Angels and demons. And this entire situation seemed like a recipe for disaster.

"I'm not giving up on you." Nina Marie reached out and patted her shoulder.

Nina Marie was quite a few inches taller than her, but that wasn't saying much considering she was only five foot three in heels.

"Once you learn more about our product offerings, I think you'll be excited to hear more about what we can do for a strong and smart professional woman like you."

"I appreciate your interest, Nina Marie, but my chief concern and responsibility is the lawsuit. So I think it'd be best if we could concentrate on that."

Nina Marie quirked an eyebrow but didn't immediately respond. Olivia followed her into another conference room, but this one was set up with multiple computer workstations around the large table. The rest of the décor matched the previous room they were in.

"This will be the legal work room for you. You should have plenty of space for everything you need in here."

"This is a great workspace." She looked around the room and was pleased by the size and technical accommodations. "I'm sure I'm going to run into a lot of factual questions as we start preparing for this first phase of litigation. Who is the person at Astral Tech I should go to with questions?"

"That would be me for pretty much anything that is detail oriented about the company or the app. Clive is good on the general business and philosophy but not so much on details. He's also not in the office everyday like I am. Matt can also serve as a resource both on the financial aspects and the spiritual ones."

"Got it." She'd never worked on such a strange case in her seven plus years of practicing law. Thankfully, she was steadfast in her beliefs. She just hoped that nothing in this litigation would require her to do things that went against her faith. Because she'd have to draw that line somewhere. And if it was a choice between her career or her faith, she'd always choose her faith.

***

Grant Baxter reviewed the document requests he had drafted one last time. He enjoyed being on the plaintiff's side of the table—even if it was for an odd client. Some wacky New Age group had retained his small but reputable law firm to sue Astral Tech—an equally wacky company in his opinion.

He didn't have any time for religion whether it be traditional or New Age or whatever. To him it was all just a convenient fiction made up to help people deal with their fears and insecurities. But if this case would help his firm take the next steps to success and keep paying the bills, then he was all for it.

He'd built his law firm, The Baxter Group, from the ground up—something he was very proud of, given all his long hours and sacrifices. Not a thing in his life had been given to him. He'd earned it all the hard way.

He couldn't help but chuckle as he read over the document requests that he had prepared. All the talk of witches and spirituality and the Astral Tech app. He'd never drafted anything like that before. His law school classes and nine years of practice had equipped him with many skills, but working on a case like this was totally foreign to him.

It wasn't like there were witches in a coven out to get him. People were entirely irrational when it came to religion. Luckily for him, he wasn't one of those people. He might be the only sane person in the entire litigation, and he planned to stay that way. One thing he was certain about. A jury was going to eat this stuff up.

"Hey, boss man." Ryan Wilde stood at Grant's door.

"What's going on?" Grant asked.

"I asked around town trying to find info on Astral Tech, but most of my contacts had never heard of them, and the few that had didn't really have anything useful to say except that they're trying to become players in the tech space."

Ryan was only about two years younger than Grant. They'd both worked in a law firm together for years, and Grant was glad that Ryan had joined him at the firm. If all progressed as planned, Grant was going to add Ryan as his partner in the firm.

"If you do hear anything, just let me know."

"Anything else you need from me?"

"Not on this. How are your other cases going?"

"I'm meeting with potential clients this afternoon on a products liability class action. It would be a good case to have."

"Keep me posted."

Ryan nodded. "You got it." Ryan walked out the door and then turned around and laughed. "I have to say, I'm glad that you're working this case and not me. I don't think I'd know how to approach it."

"Just like anything else. It'll be fine."

"If you say so. I hope you don't end up with a hex put on you or something like that."

Grant laughed. "Don't even tell me that you would consider believing in any of this."

Ryan shook his head. "Nah. I'm just messing with you."

Ryan walked out and Grant was anxious to start the discovery process and put pressure on the other side. It was one of those things he loved about being a plaintiff's lawyer. He was in the driver's seat and planned to take an aggressive stance in this case to really turn the heat up on the other side. Going through these steps reminded him how glad he was that he went out and started his own firm. He truly loved his work.

His office phone rang, jerking him back to reality.

"This is Grant Baxter," he said.

"Hello. My name is Olivia Murray from the law firm of Brown, Carter, and Reed. I just wanted to call to introduce myself. We're representing Astral Tech in the suit filed by your client. So I'll be your point of contact for anything related to the case."

Well, well he thought. Astral Tech had gone and hired a high powered law firm based in Washington, DC to defend them. "Perfect timing. I was just getting ready to send out discovery requests for documents. BCR doesn't have a Chicago office, right?"

"No, but I'm actually in town. I'm working at the client's office in Windy Ridge. So you can send any hard copies of anything to the Astral Tech office, and I would appreciate getting everything by email also." She rattled off her email address.

"Of course. And I have the feeling we'll be talking a lot. This litigation is going to be fast tracked if my client has anything to say about it. We're not going to just wait around for years letting things pass us by."

She laughed. "Yes, I know how it is. I'll look forward to your email."

He hung up and leaned back in his chair. Know thy enemy, right? He immediately looked her up on the Internet finding her BCR firm profile. A brunette with big brown eyes smiled back at him. He read her bio. Impressive, double Georgetown girl. Seventh year associate at BCR where she'd spent her entire legal career. That would make her about two years younger than him—but definitely still a seasoned attorney and worthy opponent.

Astral Tech wasn't messing around. That let him know that they took this litigation seriously. They didn't see this as a nuisance suit. Game on.

***

"Do you think Olivia's ready for this fight?" Micah asked Ben looking directly into his dark eyes.

"It doesn't matter if she's really ready, Micah. It's a battle she has to fight and the time is now. We have no one else. She's the one God has chosen who has to stand up and take this on. She has some idea that she's meant to be here. But it might take her a little time to figure out exactly what she's going to be involved with."

The angels stood behind Olivia watching over her in the conference room. But she hadn't sensed their presence as she continued to type away on her laptop and hum a tune.

"She isn't fully appreciative of how strong she is, but she'll get there," Micah said. He stood tall, his blond hair barely touching his shoulders. The angel warrior was strong but kind—and fiercely protective of Olivia.

Ben nodded. "At least she has the foundation to build upon. A strong faith that has been growing ever since she was a little girl." Ben paused. "Unlike our friend Grant."

"I'm much more worried about him. He has no idea what he's going to be facing, and he doesn't have the skills to defend himself. Nina Marie and her followers are building up strength by the day, and she'll surely want to go after him. We can only do so much to protect Olivia and Grant against the forces of evil running rampant on this earth."

"But we'll do everything we can."

Micah looked at him. "You and me—quite an angel army."

"The best kind."

"Let's pray for her now."

The two laid their hands on her shoulders to help prepare her for the fight to come. A fight unlike anything they'd ever known before.

* * *

Click here to buy TRIAL & TRIBULATIONS.

ABOUT RACHEL DYLAN

Rachel Dylan writes Christian fiction including romantic suspense and legal thrillers. Rachel has practiced law for a decade and enjoys weaving together legal and suspenseful stories. She lives in Michigan with her husband and five furkids-two dogs and three cats. Rachel loves to connect with readers.

Connect with Rachel:
www.racheldylan.com
@dylan_rachel
www.facebook.com/RachelDylanAuthor

Made in the USA
Columbia, SC
06 May 2020